TRICKS

ELIZABETH KNIGHT

Attention, please!

Don't TOUCH Sprocket!! Soul mate to Letty on loan to Dax.

Copyright 2021 © **Elizabeth Knight**

All rights reserved.

This is a work of fiction. Names, characters, places, and incidents are either the product of the author's imagination or are used fictitiously, and any resemblance to actual persons living or dead, business establishments, events, or locales is entirely coincidental.

All rights reserved. No part of this book may be used to reproduce, scan, or be distributed in any printed or electronic form in any manner whatsoever without written permission of the author, except in the case of brief quotations for articles or reviews. Please do not participate in or encourage piracy of copyrighted materials.

Knight, Elizabeth

Two Tricks

Editing: Refined Voice Editing

Cover artist: Dazed Designs

Formatting: Bookish Author Services

Chapter One
Dax

The feel of my fist hitting against flesh is such an oddly satisfying feeling. Especially when it's some cockwaffle who owes an explanation to the leader of my organization. I flicked my wrist to shake off the blood and snot I got from punching the man in the nose.

"Zeek, Zeek, Zeek," I sang as I walked around the chair he was tied to. "You do realize that the fact that I'm here dealing with this problem means you royally fucked up, right?"

"Dax... please... I didn't know who they were," Zeek begged, his eyes as wide as they could be considering they were swelling shut. Blood dripped off his chin from his broken nose and the cut under one eye.

Grabbing a handful of hair, I yanked his head back so he could look me in the eye. Even though I was five foot nothing, having him sitting brought him to the perfect level, and I used that to my advantage. "Here's the thing—I don't believe you. Two Tricks' number one rival comes to you to smuggle their dirty money out of the country, and you didn't know? The De León cartel isn't where they are today from making rookie mistakes like that."

I released his hair and took out one of my daggers from my thigh sheath, flipping it as I started my walk around his chair again. When I faced him, I grasped the hilt tight and slammed the knife into the chair right between his legs, just missing the family jewels.

"You fucking crazy bitch!" Zeek spat out, getting blood on me.

I frowned down at the blood, then looked back at Zeek, my eyes narrowing. "What did you just call me?"

Horror washed over Zeek's face as he understood what he'd done.

"I'm sorry, please, I didn't mean to call you that. I apologize. You are in no way a bitch. You're crazy—but not a bitch," Zeek back-pedaled, desperate to keep himself alive. But he had done the *one* thing he shouldn't, so I stabbed him in the meaty part of his thigh and twisted.

"FUCK ME, SON OF A BITCH! I'll admit it! You're right, I knew who they were! They gave me the payment up front and said if I proved to be trustworthy, they would double it next time. I should've never made the deal; I knew you would find out. You *always* find out."

I patted Zeek's cheek roughly, giving him a smile. "Thank you for being honest and apologizing for being so rude. Now that I have this valuable information, I'll let my boys take over."

I waved a hand to Jeff and Brian, two of my soldiers, signaling them to finish the job. I'd gotten the information I needed, and Wes had already gotten the hard data off Zeek's computer, so my work here was done. I stopped to wash my hands and arms in the kitchen sink, making sure to remove all the blood. Wouldn't want to bring any evidence of what happened here as I took the long way back on my new bike.

Pulling on my helmet, I started my new baby up and took off out of the warehouse parking lot. The feel of the wind whipping by me while the sun beat down on my skin made me feel alive, and the hum of the engine between my legs made me smile at the raw power I controlled.

Oh, I'm sure you're thinking I'm on some sleek crotch rocket in a bikini like all the other girls in L.A. Naw, not me. Nope, I needed something a little more substantial between my thighs. My baby was a stripped-down, blacked-out, Harley Iron 883, customized for more speed and power that could take me anywhere. Or at least outrun any cop that would try and stop me.

The chirp in my ear signaled that I had a call coming in, and I glanced down at my smartwatch to see who it was. The shop. Growling, I swiped to accept the call to my helmet's audio.

"This better be good," I demanded. Wes knew not to bother me on a job.

"Kimber's here," Weston stated. "She brought a friend who wants you to set up a meeting with Tricks."

Icy shock ran through my veins at this information. "I'm on my way."

Hanging up the call, I gunned the throttle on my bike, weaving through traffic as cars honked at me. Showing how much I cared, I flipped them off as I left them in my dust. Why was Devin's hoebag of a wife looking for me, of all people?

When my twin chose to join the Blackjax Motorcycle Club to be with Kimber, I lost my shit. I of course didn't find out about it until I'd graduated college, bastard having kept that tidbit from me. It was the first time I'd realized Devin kept a lot of secrets from me, and it eventually caused his death. I'd gotten my revenge on the responsible parties, but it still didn't change that half my soul was gone, never to be replaced.

Arriving, I drove right onto the sidewalk of our Main Street location. The alleyway next to the building was the perfect place for me to park my bike, and that's exactly what I did. Tugging off my helmet, I shook out my short pink hair and swung my leg over and off the bike.

Yeah, I might hate motorcycle gangs, but I didn't hold their actions against the machine.

The door chime sounded as I walked into the tattoo shop, Silver Bullet Ink, that I owned and ran with my best friend Weston. I took pride in my shop and wanted it to be an experience like none other. The walls were dark gray, almost black, with huge black and white abstract paintings I created breaking up the darkness. The waiting area had a white tufted leather couch and two armchairs with a black coffee table in the middle, and the floor contained four semi-private rooms sectioned off with black velvet curtains.

I clomped my leather boots up the steps to the open lounge area outside the office Weston and I shared in the loft, knowing that was where he would be waiting with our guests. I wanted them to know I was coming.

In one of the four vintage, blood-red leather armchairs was a woman with long black hair and bright green eyes looking up at me. Her lips thinned as she took me in, as if she disapproved of everything I stood for. I got that a lot, but ask me if I give a fuck. She was dressed in a fitted black skirt with a silk cream blouse, her black suit jacket draped over her lap. Everything about this woman reeked of money and privilege, making me dislike her instantly. She rose gracefully from her seat and walked over to me. Even without the four-inch heels she would have looked down at me, but this felt more like a power play.

"Dax, I presume. It's nice to finally meet you. I'm Gabriella Rossi, Kimber's cousin," she said, holding out her perfectly manicured hand. "Thank you so much for helping to set up this meeting. I know Two Tricks doesn't meet anyone without an introduction."

"What shit-for-brains said I would set up a meet?" I snapped as I looked at her hand, then back up to her face. "What would you want with him anyway? You're not really his type."

I glared over at Kimber, who was looking far too pleased with herself. She was your picture-perfect trailer trash. Badly bleached blonde hair, tank top that never seemed to cover her stomach, and short-shorts that were frayed at the bottom. To tie it all together, she had on worn-out, calf-high cowboy boots.

I could fucking kill her for bringing this woman to my shop. We never did business here, and she knew it. Kimber was one slippery bitch, always keeping you guessing on her motives. Apparently she'd already promised I would set up a meeting, and miss fancy pants thought I knew about it and agreed to help.... What a cunt.

Gabriella sighed and dropped her hand. "Why don't we sit?"

"No, I don't think so," I answered. "See, the thing is, my lovely dead brother's wife didn't tell me anything about this. I never agreed to help or set up a meeting with anyone, least of all Two Tricks."

Apparently, I wasn't going to get rid of her that easily.

"Well, that is problematic and certainly not starting us off on the right foot," Gabriella said, turning to sit back down. "Seems to me that I should use this chance to explain myself and see if you can help us."

Fine. She wanted to play hardball? I'm game. She had no idea who she was dealing with, and that gave me the upper hand in this negotiation.

"Okay, I'll bite," I said, sitting in the opposite chair and propping my feet on the coffee table, totally relaxed.

Gabriella looked over me again, and I knew what she saw. My pastel pink hair always caught people's eye first. Then they took in my elfin features with my almond eyes that were more silver than blue. That's where the softness ended. My nose and septum were pierced with hoops, as well as my bottom lip. My ears were gauged, large enough you could notice, but I didn't have hockey pucks waving about. The starting wisps of my chest tattoo peeked through the holes in my band t-shirt, and more tattoos covered my left arm and the bottom half of my right. The holes in my skinny jeans showed more tattoos on my legs. I was a walking contradiction of cute and deadly, all in one bundle.

And I fucking *loved it*.

"I represent a third party who would like to start doing business, but finding a way to make an offer is rather difficult," Gabriella explained.

I didn't answer right away, considering if I should give her any hope at all.

"I don't like getting blindsided in my own shop by someone I don't know, much less a person referred to me by someone I no longer consider family. Tricks doesn't need more business. Especially from a small fish."

"They are no small fish, Dax," Gabriella interjected.

I grinned. She wasn't a pushover, that's for sure. "Trust me. If they were worth the introduction, they would already be on his radar. He makes the first move, not the other way around."

"Then it seems I have taken up your time unnecessarily," Gabriella finally admitted, clearly regretting trusting Kimber by coming here to meet me. "Let me leave you with some information. Maybe you can pass it along, just on the off chance he overlooked a promising venture."

"Leave me the details and I'll reach out if something changes," I said without really committing to anything.

Gabriella nodded and reached in her purse, pulling out a business card and a manila envelope stuffed with papers.

We stood and gave each other one more assessing look before she and Kimber made their way down the stairs and out of the shop. Looking down at the card, I saw she was a lawyer—a very expensive one, if the firm name was anything to go by.

"She's legit," Weston assured, drawing my attention. He was leaning against the doorway to the office. "I checked into her while you were talking."

Wes was every girl's wet dream. His short hair was slick and styled to perfection. He had dark brown eyes that missed nothing, and full lips that begged to be kissed. He took care of himself and it showed, the outline of his toned muscles visible through his snug shirt. In my opinion, it helped that he was tatted from that strong, stubborn jaw all the way down to his big toe.

How did I know? Well, eighty percent of the art on his body was done by me.

Wes and I had been best friends since we were both in the same foster home. We managed to stick together through everything and come out on top. Wes was a kick-ass hacking genius—anything that had to do with technology was his bitch. A few times the FBI and the CIA tried to recruit him from college, but he turned them down, not wanting to leave me on my own.

"You check her accounts?" I asked, already knowing the answer.

"She doesn't seem to be on anyone's payroll we need to be concerned about. Although it looks like her law office is going to make her partner soon, which could change that."

I grinned at him, shaking my head, and slipped past him into our office. "What else did you find on her? She can't be clean if she's looking to broker a deal with Tricks."

I dropped into my chair and rolled over to his side of the large metal desk we shared. He had two monitors filled with dozens of open windows. He liked to live in organized chaos on his computer, but in the real world, he was a neat freak. Which drove me crazy when he yelled at me for leaving messes everywhere in our shared townhouse. We each had our own floors for a reason.

"It's not that she's dirty, per se... it's more that she helps some problematic people in her family." Wes sat back from the keyboard and looked at me.

Oh, this wasn't going to be good.

"The Rossi family is an interesting find. The parents are straight-laced, second-generation Italians. Emilio, Gabriella's father, is also a lawyer, but he works mostly with immigration cases. Her mother has been a homemaker their whole marriage."

I frowned, not seeing why he was so worried. I opened my mouth to ask, but he stopped me with a look. Huffing, I sat back, letting him have his way. He was driving me crazy with the dramatics.

"It's her two younger brothers we need to watch out for. Enzo and Teo. They're the leaders of the Phantom Saints."

"Wait, *the* Phantom Saints?" I questioned.

"Yup."

Fuck me!

All I could do for a moment was stare at him. If he had told me they were mobsters, I would have been prepared for that, being from an Italian family... but a motorcycle club?

My history with MCs was less than stellar. The final straw had been when Devin had to take the fall on a major drug bust for his club's vice president. It landed him in jail for two years, and while he was there, just trying to survive, he got cornered into working with a rival drug ring. The Blackjax saw it as a betrayal and turned their backs on him.

Devin would still be alive if his supposed MC "family" had taken him back.

"So Gabriella works for them. Does the family as well?" I asked, trying to figure out their circle.

"Gabriella is their lawyer and has gotten them out of plenty of charges and jail time. Dad knows but wants nothing to do with any of it. Mom might know, but she plays dumb and keeps her nose out of it," Wes answered readily.

Gabriella wasn't wrong—the Phantom Saints were no small fish. Tricks had been on the top of their "to do" list ever since wiping out the Blackjax, their sister club.

"There's no way I'm allowing a meeting with them," I declared. Tricks never worked with MCs.

"I get that, but if they really want to make a deal, the only thing holding them back is that they're a motorcycle gang," Wes countered.

"My job is to protect Tricks and the Hidden Empire," I fumed, "so what argument is there for working with them when they might just kill him if they don't get their way?"

"You're telling me Tricks would pass up the chance to have the largest West Coast MC in his back pocket because it's *dangerous*?" Wes scoffed, folding his arms over his chest. "You know this is a good idea."

Times were changing, and the Phantom Saints were making a mark, drawing unwanted attention from the competition. You could only stay the big fish for as long as you could hold it, and from what I found out today, Tricks needed to worry about the De León cartel. Having an established biker gang to act as an army would make defending the empire much easier.

"Then why don't *you* try and convince *me* this is a good idea first?" I snapped, not wanting to give in to the idea just yet.

Wes shook his head and turned back to his computer, ignoring me. There were not many people that could get away with that. Scratch that—there was *one* person who could get away with that—so I growled and stormed out the door, going down towards the studio space. I needed to sketch, punch, or fuck something, and soon. It was the only way I could process all of this without blowing up at someone.

"Hey boss lady," Jonesie called as I passed his space.

I paused, took a deep breath, and walked a step back. "What's up, slacker? You just getting set up for the day?"

Jonesie grinned at me. He was a huge beast of a man with a heart of gold. "You know I ain't no slacker. Taking care of a pregnant wife is harder than you think."

I laughed, knowing just how much work Maria could be while pregnant. "What, this is like your fourth kid, right? Why don't you leave the poor woman alone for a little while?"

"Me!?" Jonesie said, shocked. "That woman won't leave me alone. If she doesn't get her some, then I never know when she'll attack me. It's better I just give in and let her enjoy herself than fight it."

"Must be such a hardship for you," I teased.

"Just you wait. When you find the right guy and he locks you down, you'll be feeling the hardship," Jonsie said, winking at me.

"That's where you're wrong, my friend. No one man can lock this sweet ass down. Too much of a free spirit for that shit," I said, leaving him to prep for his client.

"Ha! Then hell girl, get two or three. If anyone can handle that much man, it would be you!"

Chapter Two
Dax

"Dax!" I heard Harper yell up the stairs. "I'm coming up, you better at least have a path to your bedroom for me!"

Rolling my eyes, I set down my paintbrush and turned down my music.

"In the art room!" I called back, waiting for my best friend to make her way to me.

I'll admit that I wasn't the cleanest person, but she always made it sound so much worse than it was. So what if I hated to put my laundry away and I had clean piles of it all over my bedroom floor? I knew what was clean and what was dirty, and isn't that what really mattered? Not every part of my floor in our L.A. townhouse was messy. I kept my front living area clean... mostly because I didn't really spend much time there, but hey—it counts.

I collected the brushes I was using and wrapped them in Saran wrap, not wanting them to dry out before I came back to finish. Grabbing a rag, I attempted to get the paint that wasn't already dry off my hands.

"Holy shit, Dax," Harper gasped when she walked into the room.

Smiling, I backed up and took a look at the piece before me. Even though it was unfinished, you could still see it was a man and woman wrapped in the throes of passion, unable to tell where one started and the other began.

"Girl, you are way too sexually frustrated if you are painting this shit. Good thing I can help you fix that," Harper said, bumping me with her hip.

How Harper and I became friends was beyond me. If I hadn't been forced to be her roommate freshman year, I don't think we ever would have crossed paths. She was a fellow art student, but she was into fashion and everything feminine. Her long blonde hair was curled into soft waves with one side tucked behind her ear, showing off dangly earrings. Personally, I always told her she should have been the model for all the clothes she made instead of putting them on everyone else. Being a whole foot taller than me with the perfect size two body, it would have been a done deal.

"Please tell me you're not gonna drag me to another model-infested club for one of your designer friends," I groaned.

Harper linked arms with me and dragged me to my bedroom. "Not quite. This is a newer friend of mine that's hosting a house party. She has an amazing beach house in Malibu, right off the PCH."

I looked at Harper, really wanting to say no and just spend the night working on my painting. I hadn't had inspiration in weeks, but after the meeting and argument with Wes, I was full of emotions. Seeing that I wasn't sold on the idea, Harper pouted her glossy bottom lip, her eyes pleading.

"Ugh, fine. I'll go, but if it sucks, I'm gonna leave your ass there," I said, causing her to squeal and clap her hands.

"Okay, so knowing you as well as I do, I brought you something to wear," she announced, pointing to the garment bag on my bed. "Now go shower and see if you can manage to find yourself under all that paint."

"Don't go organizing my room—you know I hate that shit," I grumbled as I stomped off to the bathroom.

Scrubbing every inch of myself until I knew Harper would deem me clean, I toweled off and set to work on my hair and makeup. As an artist, doing makeup came naturally to me. I might not do it often, but I could create with some kick-ass looks when I wanted. Plus, I knew if I didn't match up to Harper's standards, I would be forced to wash it off and start over. I learned a long time ago to just do it right the first time if I didn't want to be strapped down to a chair. Don't get me wrong, in the right circumstance I wouldn't mind being tied up—just not for makeup.

"How are things coming along?" Harper asked, poking her head into the bathroom.

"Almost done. Just finishing up with some mascara," I answered, looking over my smoky eye that made my almond eyes look more dramatic.

"Here, use this lip color. It'll complement the dress," she offered, handing me a dark burgundy color. I hardly wore lipstick since my lips were already on the fuller side. I felt like it made me look like a Kim Kardashian wannabe, but Harper kept telling me that it wasn't the same because mine were real.

Giving myself one final check, I headed to the bedroom to see what contraption Harper had designed for me to wear tonight. She loved all of my tattoos and tried to show them off as much as she could, so they often had unconventional designes.

I slipped on the dress, and I didn't hate it as much as some of the others.

It was a deep plum color that set off the pale skin beneath my ink. The skirt went to mid-thigh, molding around my ass and making it look like I had more than I did. The back was completely open, and the front crisscrossed before meeting behind my neck in a halter, leaving a bare triangle of skin that started under my boobs and stretched to my waist. Not having to worry about having large boobs made outfits like this possible and worry free. A handful was all I had, and they were going to like it if they wanted to get lucky. Finishing off with some wax to style out my hair, I was ready.

Harper came to stand next to me in my full-length mirror, taking us in. Her silky emerald-green dress clung to her in all the right places, making it look more obscene than it was. Gold chains held it to her body around her neck and low back.

"Girl, we are going to break some hearts tonight!" Harper crowed.

Shaking my head, I slipped on my black studded heels, the only pair I owned. "Come on, let's get going before I change my mind."

"You want me to drive?" she offered.

"Hell no, I know better than that. You always seem to find someone to go home with. I want a ride out of there if I need it."

"I don't always find someone to go home with," Harper mumbled.

Making it down the two flights of stairs, we reached the

main level and found Wes in the kitchen cooking. My stomach grumbled at the smell of whatever masterful meal he was making himself. I wandered over to scope it out, and my mouth watered at the shrimp scampi. Reaching out, I made to steal a shrimp, but my hand was smacked with a wooden spoon.

"Fuck! What was that for, asshole?" I yelped.

"The shrimp isn't fully cooked yet." Wes smirked and added some lemon to the dish.

"Maybe next time we could use our words instead of lethal force, ya dick," I grumbled.

"Maybe you shouldn't be sticking your fingers in someone else's dinner." Setting down the spoon, he leaned back on the counter and took me in. "You're going out?"

"You don't mind if I steal her, do you?" Harper asked, batting her lashes at him. "I'm dragging Dax to a party at a friend's place."

She always flirted with Wes, even after all these years of rejection. I knew she didn't really mean it, but who could resist a walking sex-on-a-stick like Weston?

When I bought this house and Wes moved in with me, we made a deal that we wouldn't allow sleepover guests. It was our safe place, and neither of us wanted to fear intruding on the other... It could also be that I got insanely jealous when Wes was with a girl. I chalked it up to being overly protective of him. Other than being his best friend, I didn't have any claim on him. Never once had we brought up being anything more.

"Dax is free to do what she wants. I've given up trying to stop her," Wes said, turning his gaze to me. "Call me if you need me to come get you."

Aww, Wes was just as protective of me as I was of him.

"Sure thing. We're taking the Camaro." I grinned, waving my goodbye as we headed out.

Not needing two cars with both Wes and I having bikes, we shared the matte black Camaro SS. Loving speed and danger, I of course had it tricked out. It looked lethal.

"You two act like an old married couple," Harper said, smirking as we slid into the car.

I glared at her. She kept telling me I just needed to fuck him and end the tortured need between us, and I hated it. Weston was my family, the most important person in my life growing up besides my twin. After all these years, if it was meant to happen, then it would. Since it hadn't, I was going to leave it alone. He was too important to lose over something as shallow as sex.

Harper connected her phone to the stereo and started blasting tunes, getting us in the mood to party. The drive was about an hour, but that was life in L.A. Traffic was a bitch, and people were assholes. It would have been so much faster on my bike—one of the main reasons I owned it—but Harper wasn't a fan of motorcycles and refused to let me take her anywhere on it.

"We have two missions tonight," Harper announced as the GPS told us we were almost there. "One is to get mama laid! It's been two weeks since this cat got a good scratch, and she is feeling all kinds of frisky. The second is to see if you can have fun without pissing everyone off or starting a fight."

"Do I get points if I do both?" I teased.

"I'm being serious here!" she said, punching me in the arm. "This girl has lots of high-end friends, and she could be a huge help in drumming up new business for my boutique. I don't need my angry midget best friend fucking this up for me."

"Then why did you bring me?!"

"Like I would ever go to a strange person's house without you. Bitch, please—you're my bodyguard tonight." She laughed at my threatening glare, unfazed. "Kidding. You know I hate to go to these things with people I can't rely on, and the fashion world isn't exactly known for being trustworthy."

I took a deep breath as we pulled into the large circle driveway and up to the valet stand. Leaving the car running, I took the ticket from the attendant and slipped it into my wristlet as I took in the house. The front didn't look anything special or even worthy of being in Malibu, home of billion-dollar homes. For houses off the PCH, though, the street view wasn't the front—no, the beachfront was where they made their money. Walking up to the Spanish villa-style front doors, we let ourselves in after checking in with security. Walking down a long, stone-tiled hallway, we entered the living area.

The Spanish style continued through the house, accented with a modern touch. The walls were white, and so was all the furniture, with splashes of color in soft coral. It was nothing I would ever live in—there was no life to it. Instead, it gave off the feeling of it being sterile and cold. Almost too perfect. The living room was filled with beautiful women in slinky dresses and men styled to perfection in the latest trend. I still didn't understand why their pants couldn't go all the way to their shoes. Their socks were not that interesting.

"Oh, I found her! Come on, let's go say hello to the hostess," Harper said, dragging me after her.

As we stepped out onto one of the balconies, I gasped at the view of the beach and ocean. The infinity pool on the edge of the patio made it look like you could swim right out into the moonlit waters.

"Harper, I'm so glad you could make it!" a woman—the hostess, I was guessing—said.

Unable to take my eyes off the view, I let Harper deal with the niceties.

"Thank you so much for the invite. It was so generous of you to think of me," Harper babbled, putting on her business voice. "Please let me introduce my best friend, Dax Blackmore."

Knowing I wasn't going to be able to brush off this introduction, I turned and was shocked to see Gabriella Rossi, of all women, in front of me.

Chapter Three
Eagle

I paced my office, waiting for Gaby's call to let me know how the meeting went. It had taken months of research, bribes, and breaking a few fingers to get a lead like this. We now had a line on Two Tricks' enforcer, and in my personal opinion, his lover. I had to admit that it was impressive that it took so much work to get the name of anyone worth talking to in the Hidden Empire. The Phantom Saints were done getting looked down upon by a man who couldn't even show his face.

From what we'd learned, everything was done through a third party who was picked out by Tricks. For a criminal, he sure had a lot of rules that his buyers and suppliers had to follow if they wanted to deal.

The office door opened, and three other people filed in and took seats around the room. I kept up my pacing, because if I couldn't put this energy into something I was going to explode.

"Any word from Gaby yet?" Picasso asked, kicking his feet up on the desk.

Walking by, I smacked them off and growled. He knew I hated that shit. Just because we were blood didn't mean he could disrespect what was mine. "Do I look like she's called yet?"

"Fuck, Pres, you need to have a drink or something to chill the hell out," Picasso grumbled.

I scanned the faces of the others in the room, seeing someone was missing. "Where's Cognac?"

"He had some issues with the last transaction and went to deal with it personally," Void answered, looking unhappy about it.

Stopping, I pinned him with a look. "Care to tell me why our treasurer is dealing with this and not my enforcer?"

"Seems that the situation needed a more 'gentle' approach. If I got too rough with him, then he wouldn't deal with us again, and we wouldn't have a way to transport our goods out of the state," Void explained.

"What was the issue?" I asked, even though I had a guess.

"He wanted more money for having to go behind Tricks' back," Sprocket interjected, seeing that Void really didn't want to answer my question. "Seems that something's set the crime boss off, and he's combing through his people looking for infractions. Word on the street is the enforcer is handling it personally."

"This bastard is blocking us off at every turn!" I roared, slamming my fist into the wall, cracking it. "What bastard MC fucked this up for the rest of us? There's no way we can gain any more ground without getting Tricks on our side or taking the dick out once and for all."

Picasso's phone rang out, breaking the tension in the

room. He quickly answered and put it on speaker for the rest of us to hear. "Go ahead, Gaby. We can all hear you."

"Enzo, when I tell you what happened, I need you to know I already have a backup plan ready," Gaby said, her voice sharp in warning.

"Understood," I bit out. Damn sister knew me too well.

"Using Kimber was a major backslide—the bitch lied to me. Dax hates her and doesn't trust anything that has to do with her," Gaby stated. "I left her my card and a copy of the terms that you guys came up with, but I'd be surprised if she didn't throw it out the moment I left the building."

"Is there any good news?" Picasso asked, reading my mind.

Gaby sighed. "Yes and no. Dax is definitely a good connection; she knows exactly how Tricks operates and thinks, so it wasn't a complete bust. I invited her best friend to a party I'm having tonight. I want you all to be there in case she shows up with Dax."

I had to hand it to our sister—she was a crafty bitch. I never would have thought to use the best friend.

"You sure it won't seem odd for her to just happen to show up to your party the same day you ask her for a meeting?" Sprocket asked.

"From what I gather, her best friend has no idea about this side of her life. Dax won't risk saying anything or attracting attention to why we would know each other," Gaby said, making it a nonissue. "All I need is for you all to show up and keep a low profile, and I'll see what I can do about getting her on her own for you all to talk to."

"Any chance you found a picture for us to go off of?" I inquired.

It was almost like Dax was a ghost. She had no social media of any kind, and no pictures anywhere on the internet. Almost like someone was keeping her hidden, confirming my suspicions of her being Tricks' old lady.

"She won't be hard to spot, believe me. A girl like her could never be overlooked," Gaby said, laughing.

Something about that made me grin. I couldn't wait to meet this mysterious woman.

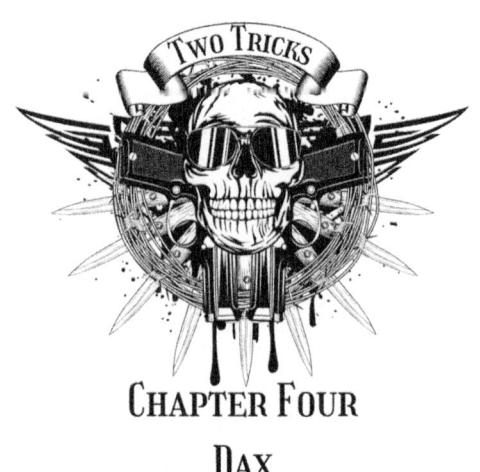

Chapter Four
Dax

"Harper, it might surprise you to know that Miss Blackmore and I have met before," Gabriella said, giving me a warm smile. "It is nice to see you again. If you could excuse me, I have a few other people that I have to go greet."

"Of course," Harper said, keeping up her smile until Gabriella had disappeared back into the house.

Then she turned on me.

"How the fuck do you know Gabriella Rossi?"

Harper had no clue of my connection to one of the biggest arms dealers and smugglers in the US. I never wanted to have my personal life and business cross, keeping Harper clean from all ties.

"We have a mutual acquaintance," I said vaguely.

Harper gave me a searching look but let the issue drop. "Let's go grab a drink."

Following after her, I searched around to see if I could find Gabriella, but she had vanished in the crowd. I pulled out my phone and texted Wes what was going on. I didn't like that I'd ended up at her house, of all places, after we had a meeting today that didn't go her way. Seconds later, I got a response that he would look into the situation, making me feel better. If she had anything hidden from us, it wouldn't be for long.

"Oh look, there's dancing on the lower patio!" Harper pointed out excitedly as she sipped her wine.

Knowing that I wasn't going to get out of dancing, I took a double shot of whiskey before I was yanked away from the bar. Passing her glass off to a server that was cleaning up a table, she tossed her hands in the air and joined the masses. Feeling the burn of the whiskey in my stomach, I decided to take Harper's advice and just let myself relax and dance. I was at a party, not a shady back office deal where I needed to worry about who was here and if they were going to attack me. It had to be just a fluke that I ran into Gabriella again. If Wes found anything, he would let me know, and I would deal with it at that point.

Slipping into the gyrating bodies, I found a space for myself and let the music wash over my skin. Since dancing was Harper's favorite pastime, I'd gotten fairly good at it over the years and knew I wouldn't embarrass myself. Letting my hips move, I watched the dancers around me. There was the typical circle of girls brushing off any attempts to have guys join, wanting "girl time." Off to the side were the solo males lurking until they could find their next victim. Then, to finish it off, were the couples where you weren't sure if they were actually having sex or not. I kept my eye on the few single guys that were watching me to see if I was open to the idea. None of them caught my eye, but I knew I was hella picky about who I let touch me. Just as one of them started to make his move, he stopped, his eyes going wide before he filtered back into the crowd.

What had chased him off?

That's when I felt someone step up behind me.

I had to hold myself back from striking out at the unsuspecting guy who was trying to dance with me. After years of looking over my shoulder, it was instinct to react first and ask questions later.

When I didn't turn or step away from the person behind me, he set his large hands on my hips and pulled me flush with his front. I could tell he was quite a bit taller than me, but that wasn't shocking. What I found interesting was he didn't say a word, just letting his body do the talking. He moved with me easily, and I could tell he had a flair for dancing.

Not every guy can "grind" on a girl well, believe it or not.

Deciding that I wanted to get a look at this guy who had managed to scare off others, I spun around and let my hands fall to his hips. Looking up at him, I could feel my body tingle, and desire flared between us. Standing before me was a Latin god with sultry light brown eyes that almost seemed copper. His thick black hair was buzzed short, showing off his defined jaw covered in stubble that I wanted to feel against my skin. Seeing me examine him, his hold on me tightened, showing off the muscles in his arms. One of them was covered in colorful traditional tattoos that I wanted to trace with my fingers and remove his t-shirt to see if there were more.

What the fuck is wrong with me? Never have I wanted to drag a man off the dance floor and find a room to show him just how much I appreciate what he was born with.

A slow grin appeared on his face, as if he knew the

effect he was having on me. His copper eyes sparkled as he stepped closer, putting his jean-clad leg between mine. Then he pulled me flush with him so I could rub myself on his thigh, getting the friction I so desperately needed. One hand moved from my waist to my low back, holding me right where he wanted me, and the other snaked its way up the back of my neck, gripping tightly and making it impossible to look away from him.

Loving the way he was controlling my body, I willingly gave into his movements. I could feel my breath speeding up as he increased the pressure on my clit, letting the lace of my thong and his jeans do the work.

Holy fuck, I was going to come right here on the dance floor in front of all these people, and I didn't give one flying fuck.

My hand slipped under his shirt, running my fingers up his muscular back, then letting my nails bite into his skin before I drew them down. He groaned and dropped his head to kiss me. He didn't hold back, biting at my bottom lip for me to let him in, and I was more than willing. His kiss was seductive and borderline painful with the force he used, but I reveled in it.

Just when I thought I was going to come all over his leg, my watch buzzed, startling me out of the haze I was in. Jerking back, I surprised my dance partner, who blinked at me, confused. Glancing at the screen, I saw it was Wes, and then the three words that would get my attention no matter where I was flashed on the screen.

"Joke's on you."

Fucking fuckity fuck balls, I had to get out of here.

"You okay?" a silky voice asked before an arm reached out for me.

Now on high alert, my head shot up, watching him as I sidestepped his touch.

"Fine," I answered and made my way off the dance floor, needing to find a place where I could call Wes and find out what the hell happened.

As I made my way across the patio, thinking I'd go inside to find the bathroom, I was jerked to a stop by someone grabbing my arm. Moving without thought, I grasped his wrist, twisted my body out of his hold, and pulled his arm up behind him, causing him to cry out.

"Fucking hell, woman, are you crazy?" my Latin god snapped, trying to pull out of my hold.

Even though I was much smaller and not as strong, I had pressure points and leverage on my side. "Why are you following me?"

"Let me the fuck go and I'll tell you, you crazy bitch," he growled over his shoulder.

The one thing I hated most was when men called women slurs. Was I acting like a bitch... yes, but he started it. That wasn't reason enough to use such language. So to show him a real bitch move, I kicked the back of one of his knees, dropping him to the ground.

"Now I know you weren't talking to me using that kind of fucking language," I whispered into his ear. "I am going to leave now, and you are going to leave me the fuck alone, okay?" I placed a soft kiss on his cheek before letting him go.

Without looking back, I made my way into the house, found a quiet hallway, and pulled out my phone, hitting Weston's speed dial.

"Took you long enough. Are you out of there yet?" Wes demanded.

"I'm sorry, *Mom*, I needed to find a place I could call

you back and not get overheard," I said, not liking how concerned he sounded.

"Damnit, Dax, you need to get the fuck out of there NOW!"

Wes was always the calm to my crazy, the peanut butter to my jelly. Opposites in everything, but together oh so good. If he was freaking out, then this was worse than I thought.

"You need to give me something so I know what to look out for," I said, opening the door to a back room, hoping it would have an exit out to the side of the house.

"The Phantom Saints are there and coming for you," Wes said, causing my anger to flare. "Where are you now? I pulled up the blueprints of the house so I can get you out."

The door to the room burst open, and five huge guys walked in, including my dance partner that I'd been humping moments ago. This time, though, he was wearing a leather vest he hadn't been before.

"Looks like a six card draw, ace high," I said, letting Wes know what I was dealing with before I dropped the phone to face the unwanted party crashers.

Chapter Five
Dax

My pulse beat in my ears, but not for the reason you would think. I was thrilled to have a fight on my hands, and a good one by the looks of it. The guys were all massive, towering over me, even the smallest built like a linebacker. I had to grin at how perfectly they fell into the biker cliché, but I had to admit—it was a good look for them.

"You're all *so* fucked," I purred, smirking at them.

"Who was that you were on the phone with? Anyone we know?" the apparent leader asked, stepping forward.

Okay, it might have helped that he had a "president" patch over his heart, which made him Enzo. The guy gave off an alpha male vibe like crazy. He was a good foot and a half taller than me and trying to use his height to intimidate me. His sharp features reminded me of a hawk or some other bird of prey, his chocolate-colored eyes tracking me as if waiting to pounce. His dark brown hair was buzzed short on the sides, but the top was long and styled straight back.

The outline of a beard along his jaw was much lighter than his hair, but somehow it worked.

My smirk turned into a full smile when I saw what he was trying to do. Mr. President started to frown, not liking my reaction to him. Too bad for this group it wasn't my first rodeo with being ambushed. Sure, no one would know, seeing as all the previous assholes who'd tried it were dead, but that just worked out more in my favor. Keeping my eyes on them, I slipped out of my heels. A broken ankle was the last thing I needed.

"This might go faster if you just tell me what you want or make a move. This posturing is getting boring," I said faking a yawn.

"Is this cunt for real?" one of the others by the door asked with a faint British accent.

My eyes snapped over to him, my temper rising at the slur. I knew it wasn't the Latin loverboy, because he already learned how much I disliked that kind of language. My money was on the scary-looking motherfucker leaning against the wall. I tilted my head, taking him in and deciding how I was going to make him eat his words.

He had shoulder-length hair that was curly and haphazard, but one side was shaved off to show his scalp tattoo. His blonde beard was thick and well looked after, but what made him scary was his icy blue eyes. They seemed to be lacking what I would call "humanity." This man could take a life and lose no sleep whatsoever. The tattoo of the word *oblivion* over his left eyebrow might have also added to his feelings about things in general. My eyes drifted to his vest, where the word *enforcer* announced his role in the merry gang of men. I couldn't have agreed more. From one enforcer to another, he was a good pick.

"Since we don't know each other I'll give you a pass, but

watch your goddamn mouth when you're talking to a lady," I said with a soft smile, but I held his eyes so he knew I wasn't fucking around.

Much to my surprise, his lips twitched like he was amused by me, which pissed me off even more. I hated to be underestimated.

Enzo took another step forward, awarding him my full attention.

"You know what we want. We had our people reach out to you," he said, stopping as my gaze landed on him.

"Ah yes, your sister did come to see me." Everyone stiffened at that. Hmm, seemed they didn't like me knowing that tidbit of information. "This is where I'm confused. I already told her that Tricks wouldn't meet with you. Tricks doesn't do business with MCs."

Enzo growled, clenching his hands into fists. *Please tell me this is where they decide to use their fists instead of talking me to death.*

Another guy stepped forward, and just by the look of him I knew he was the president's brother Teo. He had longer hair and a fuller beard, but the common features between them were undeniable.

"What can we do to change his mind?" Teo asked, seemingly the level-headed one out of the bunch so far.

Never had a group been so intent on changing Tricks' mind about the rule against MCs being allowed to do business. I decided to give something a try, because I was curious about them. I walked over to the bed and perched on the corner. Crossing my right leg over the left, I could feel them all staring as my dress rode up slightly higher. Hopefully they would just think I was tired of standing and not that it gave me better access to the knife on my thigh.

"Answer me this," I said, looking at them before I

carried on. "Let's say one of your members took the fall for your president here and ended up in jail for two years. While in jail, he was forced into working with a rival drug ring to survive. Upon him getting out of jail and coming back to the club, what would you do?"

"What the fuck does that have to do with anything?" Enzo demanded.

Giving him a bored look, I just waited, letting out a heavy sigh when they continued to just gawk at me. "Feel free to powwow if you don't have the answer, pres."

Enzo snarled, lunging forward, but Teo grabbed his arm and stopped him. I didn't even flinch, knowing that I had the upper hand in this. They needed me, not the other way around.

"Did this member get forced into taking the fall, or did he do it willingly?" a soft voice asked behind the brothers.

They parted to glare at the Thor lookalike that had spoken. His long, golden blonde hair was in a careless bun, and his intelligent green eyes met mine. The shortest one of the group, as well as the youngest looking, was road captain. Interesting. I grinned at him, seeing his train of thought and asking such an intelligent question.

"He did it himself, no coercion needed," I answered.

Enzo muttered under his breath, but the guys turned to talk in hushed tones as I looked down at my watch. I smiled, as I saw Wes was still listening to the whole conversation. *Lord, I loved that man.* He always seemed to follow whatever crazy plan I came up with. I also knew he was on his way to get me, but he was still twenty minutes out. I needed to hurry things along if I wanted to get out of here to meet him.

"We have an answer," Enzo said, interrupting my thoughts.

"Do share." I rested my head on my right hand, letting my left drape over my leg where my knife was. Never could be too safe—I was surrounded by a biker gang, after all.

"While I am thankful that this member took the fall for me and served his time in jail, I wouldn't take him back. You can't have two loyalties. If you are part of our family, then you ask us for help. You don't turn to a rival," Enzo explained.

His answer told me more than he thought it would, but sadly, it wasn't the answer I was hoping for. Even though he claimed that this hypothetical member was family, he would still turn his back on him. As far as loyalties, he was right—you couldn't be divided, and that is what drove everything that I had done since Devin died.

Standing, I grabbed my phone and shoved it back into my wristlet, not wanting to leave it behind. "Well, boys, this has been fun and all, but I can't help you."

"What?!" the icy enforcer snapped, pushing off the wall. "Listen, you crazy bitch, we played your game—"

He didn't really get to finish that statement because I was up in his face, landing a hit with my elbow into his ribs. As he bent forward, I helped him along and shoved his head into my knee and then onto the ground with a loud grunt. This seemed to break everyone out of their shock, and they converged on me. The Brit wasn't down for long, lurching to his feet with murder in his eyes. I ducked under a punch and grabbed the arm, using my attacker's own momentum to slam him into one of the other guys. The Latino with the copper eyes just watched me with a grin on his face, making no move to stop me as I bolted for the sliding glass door.

I flipped the lock on the handle and yanked at the door, but it didn't budge. Glancing down, I saw there was a second lock at the bottom of the door that needed to be released. As I was trying to get the lock to pop with my big toe, strong arms wrapped around my waist, and I was dragged back from my escape. Furious, I scratched at the steel arms trapping me against his chest, but he didn't even flinch. I lifted my legs, trying to unbalance him, but I wasn't heavy enough for that to work. Trying the next idea, I slammed my heel into whatever flesh I could land on.

"Son of a bitch!" the man swore, and his arms loosened enough for me to get a grip on my knife.

Flipping it so the blade was resting along the inside of my forearm, I sliced along his hip. With that he dropped me, and I rolled out of the way and crouched, watching them. I didn't want to kill them in such a public place. No, I was going to save that for a different night of my choosing. Roughing them up a little, though, made sure they wouldn't forget little old me.

"Fucking whore sliced me," Teo ranted, trying to stop the bleeding with his hand.

"If you want to make it out of this with only that papercut, then I would really urge you to stop calling me names. It gives me the strongest desire to stab you," I commented, adjusting the grip on my knife.

"Seems like plan B might be our best option, Eagle," Thor's twin pointed out.

I frowned, not liking that they were ignoring me and that they had a plan B. Seeing as how they weren't trying to hurt me, I didn't think their plan was to kill me, but the other options didn't seem great either. Peeking at my watch, I noticed the call had ended. Wes had to be close by now if he'd hung up.

What were the chances I could still get out of this? Two guys were blocking the exit back into the party, one was at the glass door that still wasn't unlocked, and the remaining two were slowly encroaching.

I decided to take my chances with the glass door that the fellow enforcer was guarding. He was the only one I thought could handle the damage I was about to cause with my crazy fucking idea. I feinted to the left, tricking the two brothers to dive after me that way, then sprinted off to the right. Picking up enough speed, I launched myself at the man blocking my way, making sure my knees were out in front. As I landed on him, I threw my knife at the glass door, causing it to shatter enough that when his body hit, we crashed through. I covered my head as the glass rained around me and braced for impact... but it never happened.

Arms wrapped around me, shielding me as we landed on the patio. Stunned for a moment, I didn't move fast enough to get out of his hold before an arm snaked around my neck and held on tight. I scratched, bit, and kicked, but nothing was affecting his hold. My vision started to go dark, and I knew that I wasn't going to get out of this.

This is why I fucking hated going to parties!

Chapter Six
Cognac

When she finally passed out from Void's chokehold, I scooped her up. This crazy little vixen was more challenging than we'd bargained for.

I had no fucking clue who she was when I started dancing with her. All I saw was a small, sexy, tatted woman I had to get my hands on. I never expected to find someone like her at one of Gaby's parties—she had certain rules about who she associated with.

Holding her sexy body against mine made my dick twitch. I still hadn't managed to get it to calm the fuck down from her rubbing her pussy all over my leg. Never had I been so turned on with so many clothes still on my body. I grinned at Void as he groaned, getting up off the ground and inspecting the small cuts all over his bare arms.

"That crazy—"

"Careful. You don't want to wake her up," I said, cutting him off.

"That crazy pint-size demon just tossed me through a sliding glass door!" Void said, shaking his head and staring at her with wide eyes. "Who the fuck does that?"

"Two Tricks' enforcer," Sprocket said, making his way out of the room, followed by Eagle and Picasso.

"When that snitch told us she was his enforcer, I thought he meant that she just told them where to hit. Not that she would do the hit herself," Picasso said, narrowing his eyes at the woman in my arms as he continued to apply pressure to the wound on his hip.

"We better get out of here. No telling who heard the fight or if she managed to call for backup," Sprocket suggested.

"I'll take her in her car so it's not left here for Gaby to deal with," I offered, striding through the yard to the back gate that we'd entered through.

The guys followed me silently as we checked to make sure we wouldn't be seen leaving with an unconscious woman. Eagle went to the valet and handed over the ticket that we grabbed from her purse. My jaw dropped when I saw the sexiest Camaro pull up.

"Fuck," Sprocket said, looking like he was going to come in his pants from just looking at it. "You have to agree she's got good taste."

Eagle met us at the end of the driveway and rolled down the window. "I think it's best if I get her to the compound. Not sure I trust any of you not to take a joyride in this thing."

Picasso opened the door for me, and I begrudgingly slid her into the passenger seat and buckled her in. "Can't say I trust you not to do the same, pres."

Eagle just flashed me a shit-eating grin as I closed the door and he peeled out into the night.

"We're fucked," Picasso said as we watched the taillights disappear.

"Royally fucked," Void agreed.

Chapter Seven
Dax

I rolled over, and my face was flooded with sunlight, causing me to groan and pull the pillow over my head.

"Fuck, Harper. I told you not to mess with my room," I mumbled to my bed.

Not being a morning person, I had turned my room into a cave. Working late nights at the shop and dealing with shit for the Hidden Empire sometimes kept me out until dawn. So I needed to be able to sleep late into the day, and the California sun was a worthy rival.

I groped around the bed, trying to find my phone so I could see what time it was. Unable to find it, I peeked out from under the pillow cautiously. What I saw had me chucking the pillow across the room and sitting up in shock.

"Where the FUCK am I?" I demanded to the strange room.

The room was simple with a queen size bed, plain wooden dresser, and matching nightstand. It had no personality, just white walls with nothing hanging on them. The sheets and the comforter were cream-colored, but they felt soft... so not a cheap hotel.

I slipped out of the bed, finding that I was still in the dress that Harper had made me wear to the party. Like sparks to kindling, the memories of last night came blasting back to me. I raced over to the window, hoping that I might recognize where I was.

"You have got to be fucking kidding me!" I yelled, seeing open fields and mountains.

The view was stunning, but it was nowhere near downtown L.A. Spinning on my heel, I started yanking drawers open, trying to find my wristlet that had my phone in it. I still had my watch, but it said that it was disconnected from my phone.

"Fuck, fuck, fuckity fuck, fuck," I swore and paced around the small room, pulling at my hair. "What the fucking hell is going on?!"

If those assholes thought that kidnapping me was gonna help them with Tricks, they fucked up. Bad.

"I don't know if I've ever seen something so small so angry before," a voice drawled.

My eyes snapped to the door, where I found the intrepid leader of the Phantom Saints, Enzo Rossi, leaning against the doorjamb. Behind him, I could see the cold eyes of his enforcer, watching his back like a good minion should.

Hmm... wonder what gave them the idea I might be dangerous?

"You're forgetting Gaby's chihuahua, Fifi. She was a damn angry ankle biter," the enforcer mused, moving further into the room.

I could see his arms were covered in cuts from our last encounter. It made me smile to see my crazy idea had almost worked. Next time I would have to make sure he didn't grab onto me when I sent him through a sheet of glass.

"Cute, never heard that before." I deadpanned. "Now, I'm not a genius by any means, but for me, kidnapping someone you need help from wouldn't be my first choice. Speaking from the limited experience I have, I'm not feeling all that helpful."

Enzo rubbed the scruff on his chin, taking me in as if I was a zoo animal or something. I wasn't used to being on this side of things—normally, I was the one doing this shit to others.

"See, I have this feeling that you mean way more to Tricks than people think you do. My money is on you being his old lady," Enzo said, cocking his head to the side to see if the idea fit.

I couldn't help myself. I burst out laughing at the idea that I was Tricks' lover, then doubled over when I caught the looks on both their faces. It was pure gold.

"Oh man, I haven't laughed that hard in a long time," I said, wiping the tears from my eyes. "Shit. I needed that."

Taking a moment to collect myself, I turned my back to them and looked around for something to wipe my face with. Not seeing Kleenex or anything, I grabbed the edge of the cream bedding. Once I was finally composed, I looked down to see a dark shmear from my makeup on the sheet. Not really giving a shit, I focused back on the two men, who were still looking at me warily.

"I can assure you that I'm not Tricks' type and would never be his lover," I said, letting them do with that information what they would.

The enforcer looked away and rubbed the shaved side of his head before he turned back to me. "Fine. You might not be his old lady, but we know you have his ear. You are one of the only people he lets around him regularly. That means you're still valuable, and that's good enough for us to keep you."

Keep me? What the hell did that mean?

"What Void is trying to say is that we would like for you to be our guest until Two Tricks decides he is willing to talk to us in exchange for getting you back," Enzo clarified.

Fuck!

This was so not my day.

"We tried to use your phone to call the person you talked to last, but it seems that everything has been wiped," Enzo said. "I must say, you've thought of everything to cover your tracks—even the GPS in your car is blank."

This information made me smile because it meant Wes knew what happened and where I was. He would have made sure to get all he needed before covering our trail. Moments like this were when having a hacker best friend really came in handy. Now it was my turn to do my part and get the fuck out of dodge.

"So what you're saying is that I'm your prisoner until Tricks decides to show his hand," I confirmed.

"No, not a prisoner," Enzo stated while Void nodded behind him, signaling *yes*. "A guest is more like it. You are allowed to go anywhere you like around the compound, just so long as you don't try to run away."

"Great. Well then, you should just skip to the part where I run away, you catch me, and then lock me away, because I'm not a very good 'guest,' " I pointed out using air quotations. "I'm just being honest here," I added, shrugging my shoulders.

Enzo frowned at me, clearly not used to a woman ignoring his alpha status. "You want me to lock you up?"

"God no. What I'm trying to tell you is that the moment

I have the chance, I'm outie five thousand. If I don't want to be found, I won't be," I said and perched myself on the foot of the bed. "You're going to need to give me an *extremely* good reason why I shouldn't make your life a living hell."

"Fucking little demon," Void muttered. "I told you this nice bullshit wasn't going to work."

"How does a GPS tracking anklet sound for motivation?" Enzo asked, pulling one out of his back pocket. "This one and the one on your ankle have been modified, though, to shock you with twice the force of a police taser if you cross out of the zone we set up."

I blinked a few times, looking at the thing and then down at my own foot. Sure as shit, there was a matching one of my very own wrapped around my leg. *Would Wes be able to hack into that? Probably, but I would have to figure out a way to tell him about it first.* With this, I wouldn't be able to get far before I was knocked on my ass. Being an enforcer, I'd had enough encounters with tasers to know that I didn't relish the thought of having one strapped to me at all times.

Enzo was smarter than he looked, I'd give him that.

"You have my attention," I said, looking him right in his commanding gaze.

He smirked, looking far too pleased with himself. "Did you hear that, Void? I think she's getting the picture."

"I wouldn't get too cocky there, Mr. President." From the glimmer in his eye, I could tell he liked me calling him that. "You have no idea what you signed up for, asking me to stick around. I do have a few requests though."

"Do share," Enzo said, crossing his arms as if he was preparing himself.

Oh, he is going to be so much fun to play with.

"First off, if I could get some clothes to change into. It

seems that I wasn't allowed to pack a bag for this sleepover." I gestured to the cocktail dress I was still wearing.

"I'm sure we can find some children's clothing around here somewhere," Void offered.

I took a deep breath as I ran my fingers through my hair, trying to suppress my irritation. Popping to my feet, I wandered over until I was toe-to-toe with Void, looking up into his hard, frozen gaze. He peered down at me with a smile that was more teeth than lips. It sent a shiver of excitement down my spine.

"I'm so very impressed with your observation skills, Void! I had no idea that I was small enough to fit in kids' clothes," I said in a super peppy voice, then let my face fall into bitch mode. "Yes, I'm five-foot nothin'. Also referred to as bite-size, shortstop, tater tot, half-pint, pipsqueak, shrimp, hobbit, smallfry, and my personal favorite, goblin. Now that we've covered that, let's move on, shall we?"

As I talked, his smile only grew wider and more genuine, not at all bothered with my attempt at putting him in his place.

Fine. I'd try something different since words didn't seem to be doing the job.

Snapping my knee up, I watched him crumble as I stepped back, removing my knee from his dick.

"No? How about now? Let's grow the fuck up and leave out the jokes about me being vertically challenged, okay?" I turned my back on him to continue my conversation with Enzo. "Where were we? Oh yes! Clothes would be lovely. I also need to call the tattoo shop and let them know I'll be out of town and that I need to reschedule my clients. Of course I'm happy to leave out the whole kidnapping and being held against my will part."

"Not gonna happen," Enzo said. "There is no way that

we can make sure you don't let Two Tricks know what's going on."

Point for the president.

"Okay, what if I send a text and let you approve it before it's sent? Then there is nothing to go on but the simple few words," I countered. "You're a businessman yourself, surely you can understand my position."

This was my only shot to get any information to Wes before he came in here, guns blazing, to get me. This was going to take a more subtle approach, being on their home turf. We had secrets to keep, and I wasn't going to let them use me to find them out.

"Fine," Enzo agreed. "Anything else?"

"Have you lost your fucking mind, Eagle?" Void barked, now back on his feet and motioning to me incredulously. "She all but told us she would do whatever it took to get out of here, and you're going to give her a phone?"

Enzo turned on Void, pinning the big man against the wall of the bedroom with a forearm to the neck. "Are you challenging your president?"

Void looked like he wanted to push the issue but then thought better of it. "No."

"I didn't fucking think so, because you of all people should know what happens to those who go against my judgment," Enzo said as he pulled his arm away. "Go get a burner phone so we can get this done."

As Void left the room, I could feel my eyebrows raise in shock. There was more to this president than met the eye if he could make a man like Void come to heel with just a question. Seeing this gave me a new perspective on the man before me, and I was more than pleased with the challenge it presented. Now it was my turn to poke the bear.

"Would now be the wrong time to ask you the final thing?" I ventured, stepping closer to him.

He waved a hand, gesturing for to me to continue.

"It's actually more of a statement, if I'm being honest," I said distractedly as I let my fingers run over the patches on his leather cut.

"Spit it the fuck out already," he said, the fire still in his eyes, but now for a new reason.

I gripped his t-shirt and pulled him down so I could reach him. Leaning in, I let my lips brush against his ear.

"I'm not one of your members. I'm not a hang-about you can fuck whenever you want, and you're not *my* fucking president," I whispered and kissed his neck right below his ear. He jerked away from me, eyes wild. "Don't expect me to fall in line like everyone else around you. I have my loyalties to another person, and that isn't you."

Enzo didn't speak; he just looked at me, breathing fast like he was trying to hold himself back from either killing me or fucking me. The second option I wasn't entirely opposed to—it'd been way too long since I last got my itch scratched. Just when I thought he was going to make his move, Teo walked in.

"Void said you wanted a burner phone," he said, holding it to him and totally ignoring the rampant sexual tension going on in the room.

This seemed to snap Enzo back to reality. "She's allowed to send one text, and it can't be longer than a tweet. You can be her keeper today—I have other things to deal with."

Done giving orders, he stalked out of the room. Unable to keep the smile from my lips, I focused on Teo and the phone in his hand.

"How did you get him to agree to this?" Teo asked as I took the phone from him.

"Every prisoner is allowed one phone call."

"Not prisoners who are second in command to a guy like Two Tricks. You don't get that spot by being a model citizen... no, that's for someone who has more than a few tricks of their own up their sleeve," Teo said, frowning at me. "As his counsel, we agreed that you wouldn't have any outside contact, and within fifteen minutes of talking to him, he goes against his better judgment."

"Was there a point to that statement or are we just sharing our thoughts?" I quipped as I wrote out my text to Wes. "Sorry, I just wasn't ready for us to reach 'girl talk' level friendship already."

"Damn, that's some mouth you got there, sweetpea," Teo chuckled.

I grimaced at the pet name. Not much about me was all that sweet, and I hated peas. Who decided we should eat the little green fuckers anyways?

"Yeah, that nickname isn't gonna happen," I said, handing him the phone so he could look over the text.

Teo looked over it before glancing back up at me, searching my face. *As if I would spill all my secrets that easily.* Wes and I had developed a code throughout our years of friendship, filled with inside jokes and connections no one else would make.

"That's all you needed to tell someone?" Teo asked. *"Taking a few days off, feed the cat and water the plants. Don't fuck up running the shop while I'm gone."*

I batted my lashes at him, channeling my inner damsel. "What else would I tell my manager? Like I told Enzo, I just needed to make sure the tattoo shop knew I was going to be gone. He'll contact my clients and handle things for a few days."

"Whatever. It's sent. I'll hang on to this and let you know if your manager has anything to say back," he said, slipping the phone into his pocket. "Let's get you something to eat. By then Sprocket will have found some clothes for you."

I padded after Teo, but he stopped at the doorway and turned to look at me over his shoulder. "I would also advise you not to call Eagle by his given name. He doesn't like when people call him that. Same goes for me. 'Picasso' is the only name I'll respond to."

"Duly noted," I said, not making any promises.

Chapter Eight
Dax

The rest of the house had way more personality to it than the bedroom. It was two stories, with four bedrooms and one bathroom on the top floor. The stairs led down into a large open living and dining room area. A massive leather sectional couch took up most of the space and seemed to be the place where everyone hung out. It also happened to have one of the biggest flat screen TVs I'd ever seen, as well as a pool table where the dining table should've been.

Turning the corner, I found myself looking at a long counter with five stools, marking the beginning of the kitchen, which surprisingly had the most personality. They had kept its original look with dark wood cabinets and matching wood counters. The appliances seemed to be upgraded, but the feel of the space was definitely not what I would have pegged for a bunch of bachelors.

"Sit," Teo said, pointing to a stool as he headed for the

fridge. "I'm not as skilled as Eagle with cooking, but breakfast is the one meal I can manage not to fuck up."

I glanced at the clock on the wall to see it was still much too early to be awake. I couldn't remember the last time I was up at eight, much less eating breakfast.

"Any chance a girl can get a cup of coffee? It's been a bit of a rough morning," I grumbled.

Silently, I watched Teo move about the kitchen, then he placed a mug full of pitch-black coffee in front of me. Just how I loved it.

I kept my gaze on him as I sipped my drink since I hadn't really gotten a good feel for him last night. Now I let my eyes wander over his body at my leisure. Where Enzo was more harsh and meticulous, Teo was disheveled and carefree. His brown hair had flecks of red to it and was tousled like he ran his hands through it often. His beard was thick and gave him that rugged lumberjack look. Thanks to him wearing a tank top, I devoured the black and white artwork covering his right arm.

Boldly placed right on his shoulder was a skull shrouded in shredded fabric with a large cross in the background. I knew from Wes's research that this was the Phantom Saints' mark, and I'd seen it on the back of all their cuts. Flowing down from that was smoke that broke into a sketch of a gargoyle, followed by other gothic artwork. To me it looked like the tattoo artist used someone's rough-drawn pencil sketch as reference. It was beautiful and haunting, making my fingers twitch with the need to trace over them with my own hands.

"See something you like?" Teo asked, snapping me out of my fixation. The smirk on his face gave me all sorts of dirty ideas of what I would like to do to those lips.

What was going on with me? It's like my brain decided

to turn into a horny teenager lusting after anything that was available.

"Your tattoos are amazing," I said, pausing to clear my throat. "Who did them?"

Teo looked down at his arm as if he had forgotten that he even had tattoos. "Mark Mahoney."

"Holy shit, you're kidding me!" I gasped. Mark Mahoney was a legend. "How the hell did you manage that? That man is booked out a year in advance!"

"He used to do a lot of tattooing for bikers back in the day, and when I sent him the artwork I drew for it, he found a spot for me." Teo grinned as he set a plate of food in front of me.

I snatched his arm to get a closer look before he could pull it back. The combination of Mark's tattooing skill and Teo's drawings was a perfect storm of beauty. Giving into my desires, I let my fingers whisper over his skin, causing Teo to take a sharp inhale. I flicked my gaze up at the sound, finding Teo's eyes filled with a hunger that wouldn't be fixed with food.

"You are very talented. Is that how you got the name Picasso?" I asked, relishing in his attention.

He shrugged and broke eye contact with me. "Not the most creative, but it fits."

Letting go of his arm, I looked down at the food he made me. "Um, Teo—sorry, Picasso—what is this, exactly?"

"My specialty—egg in a hole," he said, puffing out his chest.

I picked up the toast with the fried egg in the middle and took a large bite. Surprisingly, it was the perfect combination of flavors, and I hummed to myself as I gobbled down the rest. Not wanting the meal to end, I licked my fingers, not leaving any trace of it behind. Food was a surefire way to win me over, and Picasso was well on his way to accomplishing that.

Being a talented-as-fuck artist might have also helped some.

"Hated it, didn't you," Picasso chuckled.

"It was absolute shit," I teased, grinning at him. "I think you need to try that again and learn how to improve this disaster."

Without warning, a hard chest pressed to my back and hands settled on my hips, causing me to stiffen.

Fuck!

"What do we have here?" a silky voice said in my ear. "It's not every day we get graced with such a lovely sight in our kitchen."

How could I have let my guard down so easily? Normally I was extremely hard to sneak up on, but somehow Picasso had managed to lull me into relaxing my guard.

Pull your shit together, woman. You're not here to flirt and have a good time. You're a prisoner that they are trying to get information out of. LOCK IT UP!

I slid one hand over his, leaning into him and getting him to relax as he started to nuzzle into my neck. "Sounds to me like you need to raise the standard of women you let sleep over."

His grip tightened, snaking around my waist and causing me to react out of instinct. Swiftly, I grabbed his thumb and yanked it back, using it to twist his whole arm and bring him to his knees for the second time since we met.

"You really need to stop ending up like this with me," I pouted, looking down at him.

"Dax," Picasso said, walking slowly around the counter. "Let Cognac go. He's an idiot, but a harmless one."

I looked up at him, this time with my reality fresh in my mind, keeping my guard up. "He needs to learn that not every woman welcomes being touched so casually. I'm no hang-about for your club members to use."

"You didn't seem to mind so much on the dance floor," Cognac said, trying to play off the pain my hold had him in.

I frowned, letting him know he wasn't helping himself. "That was before I knew you were part of a biker gang and kidnapped me. Makes me a little more prickly than usual."

"Just think of it as foreplay and it won't sound so bad," Cognac suggested. "Some women love the excitement."

In answer, I twisted his thumb farther, causing him to land on his ass to keep me from breaking it.

"What if he promises he won't touch you again unless you initiate contact?" Picasso asked.

"Do you promise?" I asked, arching a brow at Cognac.

I found it interesting that the vice president of a renowned badass biker gang was trying to reason with me rather than force me to bend to his will. Every MC I'd had experience with acted like women were to be seen and not heard, following their command without question. Men know best, after all... *Not!*

"I promise. Only because it won't be long until I'll have you begging me to touch you, *loba*."

Growling at him, I tossed his hand away from me, not wanting to deal with him any longer. I snatched up my coffee and wandered away from them to look at the rest of the house. Farther back past the living room was another bedroom, a large master suite. I would put money on this being Eagle's room because it was as meticulous as he was. Did the rest of the guys live here too, or somewhere else? Hearing someone walking down the hall and opening the bedroom door, I braced for it to be the man himself, but it wasn't.

"You really shouldn't be here," a soft voice said.

"I couldn't agree more," I said, continuing to look over the books on Eagle's bookshelf.

"He hates for anyone to be in his private quarters. Even Picasso doesn't come in here without being invited."

I looked over my shoulder to find the last member of the five leaders. I knew better than to take his gentle demeanor at face value. You didn't end up as road captain, in charge of leading dozens of surly bikers safely to their destinations on long trips, without merit.

"Sprocket, right?" I asked, and he nodded his head. "I'll worry about not pissing off the president when he isn't holding me here against my will. Until then, I will go wherever I goddamn please."

His sharp green eyes watched me as if he could figure me out if he studied me longer. I noticed the duffle bag that he was holding and remembered that he was the one charged with getting me clothes.

"Whatcha got in the bag?" I inquired, trying not to seem too interested.

The corners of his lips twitched like he was fighting a smile as he held the bag out to me. "Found some things for you while you're staying with us."

More than ready to get out of this dress and take a shower, I took the offered duffle and headed right for Enzo's bathroom, not trusting the one upstairs to be as clean as this one would be. Sprocket made some sound of protest, but I ignored it and locked the door behind me.

The bathroom was a typical master bathroom with two sinks, shower tub, and toilet. I grinned to myself as I looked at the tub. Back home I had a huge tub with jets that I used at least one or twice a week. I loved me my bubble baths—very therapeutic—and I needed that after the past twenty-four hours. I turned on the water as hot as I could stand and let it fill as I stripped out of my dress.

Looking in the mirror, I gasped at the horrible raccoon eyes I had going on from sleeping in my makeup. Searching for a washcloth to clean up with, I started to open all the drawers and cabinets. Secretly I was hoping I would find some juicy secret or something hidden away, but nope. Just the normal bathroom shit anyone would need. Finally finding extra towels, I grabbed a set since I was going to need them anyway, then washed my face in the sink before slipping into the scalding water with a sigh.

Resting my head against the wall, I let my eyes close as I processed everything. Wes would know from the text that I was okay, held against my will, and compromised from leaving in some way. Knowing that he was out there working on a way to get me out of this fucked-up situation made this all seem less troublesome. After six years of working in the Hidden Empire, you would think I would be used to shit like this.

After my brother died, I needed to find a way to make them all pay for what they did to him. That's when Tricks came into the picture. With the Hidden Empire backing me, I was able to destroy the drug ring and the Blackjax, making sure they knew exactly why they were losing everything they ever loved or cared about. Two Tricks absorbed their business into the Hidden Empire, and it was the start of Trick's rise in the underworld. Now no one fucked with Tricks or the Empire's people unless they had a death wish. Yet here I was with a shock collar on my ankle, waiting for a rescue like some damn Disney princess.

I could just kill them all—that would solve my problem.

Take out the leadership, have Wes get this shit off me, and set the whole place on fire. I'd taken out a whole organizations for lesser offenses, so why was I even playing along with this whole situation?

The sound of the bathroom door being kicked in jarred me out of my musings. Opening my eyes, I glared at whoever decided to crash my relaxation time. Eagle stomped up to me in the tub, eyes flashing with anger.

"What the fuck do you think you're doing in my goddamn tub?!"

I let myself appreciate him for a moment before answering. Trying to hold back his anger caused him to flex his whole upper body, and it was a sight to see. His shirt was molded to his skin like it was just a little too small.

"What anyone does in a tub—I'm taking a bath," I chirped.

Enzo lunged at me, grabbing me by my hair and pulling me up so he could adjust his grip to my throat. Water splashed over the side of the tub and onto the floor, pooling around his black leather boots. I didn't fight him, wanting to see what he would do and how strong his control on his anger really was. The feel of his rough hand on my neck was more of a turn-on for me than something I feared. I could easily get out of this, but did I really want to? If he was smart, he would know that if I was killed, he'd be signing a death sentence for his whole club.

"Don't test me," Enzo snarled, looming over me. "I am not a merciful man, and you have stepped into my domain. What happens now is your doing."

Just when I thought I might have misread the whole situation, Enzo's lips crashed into mine. His hold on my throat held me against the wall as he took from me what he wanted, showing my lips little mercy—and I loved it.

CHAPTER NINE
DAX

I moaned under his harsh attention, my body flooding with need. Wanting him to know that I was all in for where this was headed, I wrapped one leg around him, tugging him closer. Dropping his hand from my neck, he grabbed my ass and lifted me, pinning me against the wall with his hips. Clutching at his shirt, I gave as good as I got, nipping at his lips hard enough to make him hiss. One hand reached up and tweaked my nipple harshly, making me cry out, his mouth smothering my sounds.

Turning, he plopped me down on the counter and ripped off his shirt. The Phantom Saints symbol was boldly tattooed on the middle of his chest. I let my fingers wander over his skin, feeling the smooth muscle shifting under my touch. Seconds later he was naked, and his dick stood proudly on display. I'd seen a fair share of cocks in my day, but this man made me wonder if it would even fit into my small body.

Enzo stepped back into me, letting his dick rest against

my stomach. "I don't rape women, no matter how pissed off I am, so I'll give you two seconds to push me away and leave. Otherwise I am going to fuck you so hard you won't be able to walk, let alone run away from me."

I shuddered at his words, the thrill of them making me even more wet than I already was. My brain screamed that we shouldn't do this, that it would cloud my judgment to let him take me, but I pushed away my worries. I'd already known what choice I was going to make the moment he entered the bathroom. These men used women; they didn't keep them. So I was just going to follow their example and take what I needed.

Placing my hand on his chest, I pushed him back enough that I could slip off the counter. I looked up at him, but he closed his eyes and looked away, expecting me to leave. Instead, I grasped his dick and gave it a firm squeeze, pumping it a few times and making him growl. I could feel the sound of it coming from his chest, and it pushed me to make him do it again. Dropping to my knees, I held his dick in one hand and braced my other on his hip. I peered up at him and gave him a wolfish grin before I took him into my mouth, quick and deep.

He was so large that I couldn't manage it all, but I didn't let that stop me from trying. Working him with my hand and mouth, I relished the groans that were coming from his throat. He grabbed a handful of hair and tried to force my head down on his dick, but I reminded him who was in charge by letting my teeth scrape along the thin skin, making him flinch. Pulling back, I let his dick pop out of my mouth and looked up again.

"Sorry, Mr. President, but you're not gonna get off that easy," I said as he growled at me for stopping.

Apparently not liking my answer, he grabbed me by the

throat again and bent me over the counter. He shifted so he was holding me down with a hand between my shoulders as he lined up behind me. I watched in the mirror as he thrust into me, not even checking to see if I was ready for him. I cried out my pleasure, feeling his fullness between my legs. If he hadn't pinned me down, I'm not sure my legs could have supported me. One hand on my hip, he thrust into me, the sounds of flesh colliding and panting filling the air. I tried to find something to hold onto as he slammed into me, setting my body on fire.

Never having been shy when it came to sex, I had experimented a fair share, and the blurred line between pain and pleasure was always a favorite. Being a badass all the time made it difficult to find a guy to fuck you into oblivion that wasn't just a little scared of you. Enzo didn't give a fuck who I was in this moment, and I was living for it. Feeling the build start, I pushed back on his thrusts, forcing him even deeper.

"Fuck yes!" I yelled when he slapped my ass.

Enzo bent over so his chest covered mine as he kissed and bit at my neck. "You will learn your place here, little hellcat, even if I have to show you every day where it is." Surprising me, he bit down harder on my shoulder as he sped up his thrusts.

I screamed as my orgasm took me under, causing me to shatter under him. Not caring, he powered through it, keeping up a pounding pace and sending me into another release. This time he followed me, clutching my hips and holding me tight against him as he moaned above me. I lay limp on the counter, a sheen of sweat covering my body as I tried to remember how to breathe. Enzo pulled out of me and scooped me up to set me on the toilet. Silently, I watched him as he drained the tub and started the shower.

Coming back to me, he picked me up like I was a doll and stepped under the water. He set me on my feet but held me against his chest, steadying me. The water helped to clear my mind of the orgasmic bliss and bring me back into my body. I moved to stand on my own and put space between us, but Enzo's fingers dug into my hips, holding me where I was. I looked up at him, confused, and was shocked to see a look of possessiveness in his eyes. A new tingle of fear curled into the pit of my stomach. Never did I think that this volatile president of an MC would see what we did as anything other than purely physical.

"Enzo, you need to let go of me," I said, putting a warning edge to my voice.

Enzo caught my chin, forcing me to look at him, his painful hold almost causing me to whimper. "Don't let me hear you say that name again if you want to avoid me testing out your new accessory."

Like a switch had been flipped, his sexy dominance turned into alarming reality. I was always on the edge of a knife with this man, and I couldn't afford to keep forgetting that. Sex would only bridge the gap so far when he didn't see women as equals. That fact was always going to cause us to clash.

I sighed, causing him to frown at not getting the reaction he'd expected. Slapping his hand off my face, I yanked the arm back behind me, causing him to pitch forward. This allowed me to wrap my other arm around his neck and twist, rolling him out of the shower and taking the shower curtain down with him.

"Test that shit on me and see how that goes for you, Enzo." I stepped over him, grabbing my towel and duffel before marching out of the bathroom.

I paused when I saw Cognac and Picasso in the living

room, watching something on the TV. Both of them looked over at me when I entered the room. Picasso's eyebrows rose in shock at seeing me wet and in a towel. Cognac, on the other hand, took his time looking me over as if he was trying to burn it into his brain for later. Huffing out a breath, I held my head high and walked right past them and up the stairs. I still really needed a shower, so I headed for the bathroom first.

After taking the quickest shower of my life, I looked through the bag of clothes. Surprisingly, Sprocket had gotten things that would fit, even if the shorts barely covered my ass cheeks. The black short-sleeve shirt was soft and hung off one shoulder. Thankfully, I didn't really need to wear a bra, and since I didn't see one in the bag, I went without. Slipping on the pair of flip flops, I made my way back to the bedroom I woke up in and found Picasso laying on the bed.

"You've had a very busy morning, haven't you?" Picasso said, not opening his eyes.

"Another reason I don't like to be up before eleven. Too much time to get into trouble," I grumbled, putting the other clothes from the bag in the dresser.

"Good to know for the rest of your time with us since it seems like you're going to stay a while," Picasso said as he sat up. "Can't say I've seen a woman come into our house and make such a lasting impression in such little time."

"It's my competitive nature." I shrugged, trying not to grin.

I literally just fucked his brother. I shouldn't be flirting with him if I don't want to be thought of as a hang-about. Right now I'm not acting any different than them.

Picasso climbed off the bed and waved for me to follow

him. "Let's get you out of the house before you fight or fuck someone else and I never get to give you the welcome tour."

I couldn't help myself and laughed as we made our way down to the front door. The heat of the summer hit me as soon as I stepped out onto the wrap-around porch. It'd be lovely to spend time on under different circumstances. Picasso headed off toward the massive metal cattle barn, and I followed him but continued to take in the surroundings. Scattered around the property were simple ranch houses like this was some type of commune. In the main hub of the property was a gravel circle drive, on the left there was a repair shop with three garage doors open, showing off the work going on inside. To the right was the long driveway leading out of the compound to the main road that was miles away.

"Sprocket runs the shop and works on all of our bikes. We do custom jobs for other people, but that's at our location off the compound. This here is for Phantom members only," Picasso said, seeing where my gaze had strayed. "The old cattle barn ahead of us has been converted into the clubhouse. That's where everyone hangs out when they're not on the road or working."

When we reached the clubhouse, he pulled open one of the double doors for me, and I raised a surprised brow as I passed him into the dark dwelling. There were no windows, and the large barn doors were not pulled open. Once my eyes adjusted to the dimness, I saw that it was everything I would have imagined a biker hangout to be. A bar ran along one wall with a few guys scattered along it, drinking. Others sat on the mismatched couches that were placed in clumps around the large space. A few pool tables were scattered about, not being used, along with some dartboards on the wall.

"Is this a clubhouse or a seedy dive bar?" I asked, wrinkling my nose at the smell of sweat, sex, and stale beer.

"Can't it be both?" Picasso asked, winking at me. "We let the members decide what the place looked like since it's really for them to spend time in."

"I'm guessing your brother has control over what happens in the house? It's way too orderly for five bachelors to be living in." I said as I wandered over to the bar.

Picasso chuckled, leaning against the bar as I sat down on one of the stools. "Noticed that, did you? Yes, Eagle likes order and control in all things and people. He allows this to be the one area he doesn't rule over."

The bartender saw us and headed in our direction. He had to be in his sixties, grey hair cut short with a long grey beard that was braided. His skin was tan and wrinkled, and his tattoos had a bluish hue, showing they were almost as old as he was.

"Surprised to see you here so early in the day, Picasso. What can I do for ya?" he asked, ignoring that I was even sitting here.

I bristled at his slight. Yes, Picasso was vice president, but it's considered good manners to say hello to someone sitting at your bar. Fuck if he'd be getting a tip from me.

"Pinky, this is Dax," Picasso said, gesturing to me. "She is a guest of Eagle's for the foreseeable future. I wanted to make sure that I introduced you so you can keep an eye on her if we're not around."

The older man looked me over with his judgment-filled eyes. *This fucker better not think I'm Eagle's flavor of the week. It happened once and never will again.*

Reaching out a hand, I gave him a bright smile. "Nice to meet you, Pinky."

He just looked at my hand but didn't take it.

Okay, playing nice wasn't going to work with this crusty old prick.

"Pinky, I would really hate for us to get off on the wrong foot," I said, dropping my hand and leaning across the counter. "You see, I have this terrible impulse control problem when it comes to people I don't like."

"Why would I give two flying fucks about a bitch like you not liking me?"

"Dax..." Picasso tried to stop me, but I did warn the guy.

Darting my hand out, I seized Pinky's braid and yanked downward, slamming the older man's face into the bar. Pulling myself up on the bar, I sat next to the dazed biker and looked down at my nails like I didn't notice every eye in the clubhouse watching.

"Now Pinky, I get that you're old, and maybe that senile brain of yours isn't working as quickly as it used to, so I'm going to go easy on you," I said, swinging around so I was facing him. "Call me a bitch or any other name that is demeaning to women, and you will be eating out of a straw for the rest of your miserable life."

"Fuck, you're perfect for them," Pinky said, his words muffled from trying to stop the bleeding from his nose.

Turning to face the rest of the men in the clubhouse, I raised my voice. "Hope y'all took good notes, boys. I hate repeating myself."

Hopping off the counter, I made my way out of the barn knowing that Picasso would follow after me.

"Dax, we really need to talk about your people skills," Picasso said when he caught up to me.

"Really? I thought that went well," I chirped and headed off down the driveway, wanting to get a feel for the layout of the compound.

I heard him groan behind me, making me wonder how

long his patience with me would last. Typically I wasn't this volatile, but I felt like it was the right part to play in this situation. Better to have them wondering what I would do next than to be predictable. That made you vulnerable to being tricked, and that wasn't in the plans for me.

"Where do you think you're heading?" Picasso asked as I kept walking.

Peeking over my shoulder, I shrugged. "No idea, just felt like going for a walk. I'm feeling a little stifled at the moment. I'm not used to having someone follow me around all the time."

Ignoring my grumbling, Picasso gestured to the land around us. "This is an old cattle ranch that we took over. So most of it is open pasture that butts up to the mountains. We own the land right up into the foothills, a little less than eight hundred acres, I think."

A thousand acres. That's a shit ton of land to have. I knew Wes looked into the stability of the Phantom Saints, but I hadn't ever looked over that information. It made me think that I should start looking over anything Wes sent me about groups we were keeping our eyes on.

We wandered the property in silence for a while, just enjoying the sunshine.

"I hate to cut this short, but I have to get you back to the house," Picasso said bringing me back to the present.

"Oh? Some secret squirrel meeting that you can't let the enemy know about?"

"No, just church. Only members can attend."

"Ah, so it's that I'm a woman," I concluded knowing that no women are allowed in their super-secret meeting they call *church*. "Why is it that MCs just seem to have the inability to understand it's the twenty-first century and not the fifties? Housewives have been freed from the shackles of the kitchen and secrecy, you know."

"We are not like that at all. If we were, I would have punished you for what you did in the clubhouse," Picasso said defensively.

I stopped on the steps up the porch to the house so I was eye level to him. "If Eagle had been there, he would have. Just because you treat women with respect doesn't mean this club does. Everyone takes note from the president on how to act."

"Don't you fucking talk about my brother like that!" Picasso snapped, getting right up in my face. "He takes care of everyone in this club, and I won't stand for you slandering him."

Here I was thinking he might be the nice one out of the group. Seeing the tinge of crazy going on in his eyes, I decided for once to keep my mouth shut on the subject. I knew Picasso had been too perfect, but now I knew what made him tick.

Don't fuck with his brother.

He took a deep breath and seemed to shake off his rage. "Stay here, relax, take a nap, whatever you want—as long as it's in this house. Remember, we can tell exactly where you are, and I am changing the geo-fencing so you will get shocked if you leave the porch. I'll be back after the meeting."

Chapter Ten
Picasso

I watched her walk into the house, not trusting that she would believe me about the ankle tracker. This small woman packed more punch to her than a category five hurricane, and she was going to blow through this place if we didn't get her on our side. Making my way back to the clubhouse, which was now full of all the men in our club, I hurried over to the bar where I knew Eagle and the others would be waiting for me.

"She at the house?" Eagle asked, his phone in hand.

"You tell me—you're the one tracking her," I said as I sat down next to him. "Don't forget to switch to the small fence around the house. Let's see if she'll listen to my warning."

Void scoffed as he took a sip of his whiskey. "That little demon, she won't listen to anyone but Two Tricks. It was a mistake to bring her here."

"Not here," Eagle snapped. "We will talk about this when this is over. Phantom Saints leaders don't argue in front of the family."

I scanned the room and saw that everyone but the few we knew wouldn't be here were ready and waiting. Eagle stood from his stool, took his gavel, and struck the bar soundly, alerting everyone that church was now in session.

"Today will be quick. Not too much to go over, but what we do have is not great news," Eagle said, his voice booming through the space. "The mover we had is squeezing us for more money because they don't want to be caught dealing behind Two Tricks' back. We are scouting out new options for this problem, but if anyone hears about more of our connections getting cold feet, we want to know. Business is fine, and we have other areas that Tricks has no hold over, so be assured there is still work to be done and money to be made."

The room rumbled with talk and uncertainty as they took in that information. Our group had been around for ten years and survived the loss of our sister club, the Blackjax, six years ago. This was another bump in the road, but it would be one that we could weather if Eagle would get out of his own way. As he said, we didn't need the Hidden Empire's help to grow, even if it would make it happen faster— damn Mad Dogs trying to box us in.

"On another note, I have a guest that you will be seeing around the next few weeks. She is off limits." Eagle gave the men a hard look. "I need her to be on our side to broker a deal, and she wants to see how things run on our end. Let's show the little lady just how the Phantom Saints became the top dog on the West Coast," he said with a smirk that had the guys getting to their feet, hooting, hollering, and whistling their agreement.

I was shocked to hear Eagle talk about her in church. We had all agreed that we would have her keep a low profile and let them think she was his newest side piece. Had something changed on his end? Why didn't he tell us? We never made choices like this alone. We always worked as a team.

"Now I'll open the floor for any new business," Eagle said and sat, looking over the group of men.

Tapper stepped forward, and the room fell silent again. "One of my snitches said that one of Tricks' competitors on the East Coast was getting ready to make a move. Word on the situation is that he let his enforcer go too far and they killed his son without provocation."

My brows shot up my forehead, and I looked over at the rest of the guys. I could tell from their faces that none of us had heard a peep about this, and we'd been keeping our ears glued to the ground for any news when it came to Tricks and Dax.

"Does your snitch know the name of the rival?" I asked.

"They didn't know, but it happened last year. It just took them a long time to find out it was a hit by Tricks. He didn't leave his usual calling card of a double ace playing card," Tapper said, shrugging his shoulders.

Why would he have a hit then not take credit for it? That made no sense—if it's a rival, then you make sure they know you won. Was it a rogue hit? Did Dax act out on her own and try to cover it up?

"Bring your snitch in, we want to talk to him," Eagle said, giving me a look. He didn't think it added up either. "Anything else we need to know?"

When no one spoke up, another rap of the gavel sounded, and the men drifted off. Eagle signaled us to follow him to the office in the back of the clubhouse, and everyone sprawled out into their usual spots as I shut the door and locked it. I trusted every member of our club, but that didn't mean I would be stupid. The things we talked about in here we sure as hell didn't want anyone else knowing about.

"Do you really think she would take out a rival's kid without claiming it?" Sprocket asked, chewing on this thumbnail.

"Abso-fucking-lutely I believe that," Void said. "All he would have to do is call her a bitch to get punched. Imagine if he called her a twat or something. From what I've seen in the twelve hours she has been around, that girl is a loose cannon."

Cognac just chuckled. "You're just pissed because you got your ass handed to you twice by our little *loba*."

Void snarled, baring his teeth. "Don't you fucking name her. We can't keep her."

"Why not? It seems our leader might have changed his mind on that," Cognac said, winking at Eagle.

He was one of the only people I knew who could get away with shit like that. When Eagle didn't deny the accusation, the room paused, and we all looked at him. He was sitting behind his desk, leaning back in his chair, rubbing his chin, not even paying attention to what we were saying.

"Eagle," I called out, grabbing a pen from his desk and tossing it at him.

Immediately he glared at me, but then he settled back and focused on us. "I might have been short-sighted on how to deal with Dax."

"Fuck," Void said, getting up and grabbing the whiskey off the shelf to pour himself another drink.

"What's your new plan?" I asked, cutting off Cognac from voicing whatever asinine thing he was about to say.

Eagle leaned forward, resting his elbows on the desk, telling me that I wasn't going to like this. "Instead of trying to get Two Tricks to play ball with us, what if we took his move and just took over?"

"Run that by me again?" I blurted, not sure I was hearing the crap that was coming out of my brother's mouth.

"We have his second in command, whether she likes to admit it or not, so we turn her against him. We have rivals sniffing around, so he will be distracted, and not having his enforcer will cripple him," Eagle laid out.

"It's really rather smart," Sprocket agreed. "Dax already has all the information that we could need to take him out. If we get her to side with us, then it's game over for him."

"Look guys, we have no idea what shit he has on her," Void countered. "There has to be some reason that she joined him in the first place. Now that we know he isn't her lover, what other reason would a woman have to be at his beck and call?"

"God Void, you really are an idiot sometimes," Cognac said, shaking his head. "Why can't she be in it for the same reason we would be? Power. She is, for the most part, untouchable, rich, and way fucking smarter than I think we give her credit for."

"I have to agree," Sprocket said. "Dax isn't the type of woman that wants to be taken care of. She can handle her own shit just fine. To me, it would be her freedom that he's got over her. He could take away everything she has and leave her with nothing."

"What about her shop?" I asked.

Cognac grabbed his tablet from the desk and flicked it open. As treasurer, Cognac was our stock market money-making magician. He had a way of making the simplest moves that had the biggest impacts. He also knew his way around technology better than any of us did, so we left him to do research with Gaby.

"From the legal paperwork that Gaby found for the sale, it looks like she took out a loan for it with a co-signer, Weston Price. The odd thing was that it only took her two years to pay off a fifty-thousand-dollar loan. This was around the same time that Two Tricks was really making waves in the industry," Cognac said, scrolling through the info.

"Okay, so she has another source of income, but no matter how good a tattoo shop does, it doesn't pay as good as Tricks has to," I said, frowning. "This doesn't help us with getting her to turn on Tricks, though. If we take over, then we don't really need her, do we?"

Eagle scratched the scruff on his chin as he thought. "If this plan works, it will only work with her being a part of it. This whole thing could be smooth sailing if we have a familiar face for them to trust."

"That still doesn't tell us how we are going to get her to turn on him," I pointed out.

"Simple. We make her fall in love with us," Eagle said as if we all should have thought of it.

Void shot out of his chair and slammed his fist on the desk. "Are you out of your goddamn fucking mind, Eagle?!"

Eagle just looked up at him with an expression I knew all too well. If Void didn't back off, he was going to end up with a broken bone or two. My brother did not tolerate others second-guessing his judgment. There was a reason he was the president and had stayed in that position for so long. The five of us were close, brothers in all meanings of the word, but that went out the window if you were going to challenge him.

"Sit the fuck down before I make you," Eagle barked,

his eyes narrowing on Void. "This is twice in one day I've had to tell you to stand down. There won't be a warning next time."

Void froze, knowing he had made an epic mistake, and sat down without another word.

"Anyone else care to chime in on how they feel about this?" Eagle asked, looking at all of us in turn. "I remember the pact we made when we started this club. No woman is coming between us, turning us against each other. If we do this, then we do what we always planned. I know you all have a thing for her. I'm giving you the go-ahead to act on it."

"Eagle, that pact was never meant to be taken seriously," I said, totally blindsided by the turn of this conversation.

Grunting at me, he scooted back from his desk and walked over to the wall safe. He sorted through a few things, then pulled out a folder that was warped and stained from age. Flipping it open on the desk, he pulled out the original handwritten rules we made for our club ten years ago and read the section aloud.

"The club's needs come first and foremost. As leadership, we are brothers united, letting no one get between us. We all agree not to take an old lady unless we all share the same woman. If we do not find someone who can do that, we will only deal with hang-abouts and other flings. If one of us takes a woman, we are all given the right to show our interest, but if they reject one of the leadership, then that brother breaks off all attachment. If they fail to do this, it gives the leadership grounds to remove this brother from his position."

"God, we were idiots when we wrote that shit," Void said, hanging his head. "So what you're really telling us is that you have a major hard-on for this woman and need a reason to keep her around long-term."

"I'm pretty sure if she had let him, Cognac would have fucked her this morning over the kitchen counter. I'm not the only one with a hard-on for her, and you know it," Eagle retorted, sitting back down in his chair. "Look, if this all works out, it's a win-win. We fuck Tricks over and get the girl."

Sprocket's fidgeting drew our attention. Typically he was the stoic one of all of us, so this whole thing must've really gotten under his skin. "You're not factoring in the possibility that she might not want all of us. What happens if we try this and she tells us all to fuck off?"

"This can't seriously be happening," Void grumbled, turning to Sprocket. "I haven't seen you show any interest in a woman for so long, I thought you might actually be gay. What about her has you all wound up?"

"I might have a clue," Cognac said, grinning as he slouched in his chair.

Void looked at him with disgust. "For you they just have to be breathing and have a pussy for you to stick your dick in. You're actually interested because she isn't."

"Can you blame me? It's oddly refreshing to end up on my knees for a change," Cognac said, getting a dreamy look in his eyes.

"Anyway," I interjected, trying to direct this conversation into something purposeful. "Sprocket makes a good point. Let's say we try this and it goes nowhere. What then?"

We all turned to Eagle, waiting for his answer. "Then we go to the original plan. If she won't help us willingly, then we will force her to tell us the good old-fashioned way."

"No, absolutely not!" I yelled, then pointed a finger at the desk. "And before you even try to put me in my place, pick up that sheet of rules and tell me what number ten says."

Eagle growled at me, but he had no leg to stand on, and he knew it. If he was going to use the "original rules" ploy, so could I. Seeing that he wasn't willing to admit his disregard for rules that made it harder for him, I turned to the others. "Anyone else remember what rule ten is?"

"We don't harm women or children, they are off limits," Sprocket said softly. *"Because everyone has family that can be used."*

Eagle gripped the arms of his chair until it started to creak under the strain. "Well then, little brother, how are you okay with us having kidnapped her and keeping her here?"

The bastard wasn't willing to fight fair on this, was he?

"None of us are hurting her. If she steps out of line and gets herself shocked, that's on her. When we decided this, we always planned to let her go—torture and strong-arming her was *never* on the table," I explained through clenched teeth.

"Picasso's right," Cognac said. "If we break this rule, then we might as well have no rules. We created this club to protect people like us that didn't have anywhere to go, people who needed a family. Phantom Saints are different, and that's what makes us stronger. That's what's earned us respect when other MCs get looked down on."

As we talked, Eagle softened, showing me that he was listening. We wouldn't let him bully us into making a choice that would affect this club negatively. It was the whole reason we were all in this together—no one man can do it right.

"Fine. Then I say we try my plan, and if it doesn't work, then we decide on plan B. We will get to know her and the situation better, get more information to go on," Eagle said, coming to a compromise.

"I'm in like Flynn, don't have to ask me twice," Cognac said, grinning excitedly.

I sighed, knowing I couldn't deny my brother the chance to see if this woman was what he hoped. Yes, we always said that the club came first, but for me, Eagle was top priority. And before I blew up at her, I'd felt like we had a real connection. The time we spent together today made me feel like this might not be such a crazy idea. If we ended up not being lovers, I could see us being friends. "Alright, we'll try your idea."

"Fuck me, I'm in. That little demon might be the only woman who isn't too afraid of me to love me," Void said, rubbing the shaved side of his head. "But believe me when I say that little demon is going to be more work to handle than you guys think."

That left Sprocket. This would only happen if we all agreed. If he said no, then we wouldn't address it again.

Then a smirk crossed his face, and I knew his answer. Finally something interesting was going to happen around here.

CHAPTER ELEVEN
DAX

Knowing Picasso was watching me, I entered the house without another word. These idiots. Like I was upset about being left alone, *unsupervised*, in their house. Puh-lease. I looked around the living room, trying to decide where to start gettin' my super snoop skills on. Then I decided it was smarter to work top to bottom—the lower level was easier to have access to, even if they were all around.

First I stopped by the kitchen to grab a drink out of the fridge. Yanking it open, I found that it was fully stocked with real food—it almost looked like Weston had just gone shopping at our house. Spotting a row of beers, I snagged one and popped the top.

"Fuck it, not like I'm going anywhere that I'd need to be sober," I muttered to myself as I noted the time—noon—and wandered up the stairs.

At the top of the stairs was the first bedroom. Tossing the door open to see which asshole put himself in line to be killed first, I felt slightly let down with how sparse it was. Did someone actually sleep in here?

The room was painted a dark gray, and the queen size bed was like a sea of black fabric. Whoever slept in here clearly didn't make their bed in the morning.

Who was I to judge? I didn't ever make my bed either. Stepping further into the room, I saw hanging on one wall was a huge poster advertising for a UFC fight. Standing dead center, fists up and piercing icy-blue eyes staring me down, was Void. Only on the poster was his given name—Lachlan Kinsley. It was dated twelve years ago for a championship in New York. Apparently, Lachlan had been a big deal in the fighting world before he became part of the Phantom Saints.

It seemed that in the years that passed, Void liked to travel on the light side. Opening his closet, I found it half full of random boxes containing more fighting memorabilia. Nothing was hung but a single leather jacket that was well-loved. Leaving the closet, I rifled through his dresser, and other than the fact he wore fitted-style boxers, I didn't discover anything interesting. The only thing left in the room besides a punching bag hanging from the ceiling was a side table. Pulling open the one drawer, I found condoms, a gun, a box of bullets, and a picture of a rich couple with a young boy. Looking closer at the boy, I saw the telltale eyes that gave him away. They matched his mother's perfectly, but in every other aspect he was just like his father. When I flipped the picture over, written on the back was *Summer holiday in Cotswolds*.

"I was right, it is a British accent!" I grinned. Typically I sucked at guessing accents, and his wasn't very strong to my ear.

Putting the picture back, I closed the drawer. At least I

knew where to get a gun if I needed it now. Looking around, I made sure everything looked like it had when I walked in, but there hadn't been much to fuck with to begin with.

Off to the next room, which I was pleased to find was way more interesting.

I knew right away it was Cognac's room from the burgundy silk sheets alone. The king size bed was the focal point of the room, but what caught me off guard was that one of my paintings hung above it. I had an art gallery that sold them for me, and because it was a hobby, I never listed my name on them. In the art world, I was known as "The Pink Lady." This one had in one of the first batches I had sold, so Cognac had been a patron of mine for a while. The image was of a woman in a red slip nightgown sprawled across a white bed, her black hair swirling around her. What made this painting truly pop was the fact it seemed like the woman was staring right into your soul, asking for you to fuck her raw. It was little wonder why he had picked this one to have over his bed.

I wandered over to the desk, which was covered in paperwork around a laptop. I popped open the laptop, but of course it was locked, and I didn't have Wes on speed dial to help me unlock it. Moving on, I skimmed over the papers, discovering they were just a bunch of financial reports on stocks. This was so not my wheelhouse—it seemed like another language to me. What did catch my eye was a handwritten list of names in a notebook. Names that I was very familiar with because they were my people. Each of them I had groomed to help me on my enforcement team.

Was this how they found me?

Flipping through the notebook, I found more information about me and the leads they had connecting me to

Tricks. They were good, I had to give them that, but the one person who started the manhunt for them was Kimber.

"I'll kill that fucking bitch," I growled, feeling my anger grow. Brother's widow or not, she'd crossed the line.

Nothing else on the desk or in the drawers gave me much to go on. Still bitter at being betrayed, I stormed down the stairs, tossed the beer bottle into the sink, and scoured the kitchen for something stronger. After the third try, I struck gold. Every shelf in this cabinet was full of every type of liquor I could think of. I grabbed a bottle of brandy and a glass, taking them both with me back upstairs.

I passed the room I'd woken up in and the bathroom, coming to the last door. It was slightly ajar, so I nudged it open with my elbow and paused before walking in. The whole room looked like an engine threw up everywhere. Parts and tools were scattered all over the floor and rested on any flat surface that could be found. The bed was a small twin mattress on the floor that was shoved in the corner. Car-part company signs were hung on the walls, along with posters of different motorcycles.

"Yup, not even gonna try," I muttered, backing out of the room. I might get tetanus from something in there.

This time I didn't bother shutting the door. They weren't hiding anything in that room. Heading back down, I went for Eagle's room, having saved it for last. Picasso must have a room elsewhere on the compound, not having seen any other rooms in the house.

Back in Eagle's room, I sat in the armchair next to his bookshelves and set my brandy on the side table after pouring a glass. Shifting, I looked over the room again now that I had the time to do it at my leisure. It was all very modern but masculine. He had expensive taste and liked the finer things, even if he didn't let it show openly.

The bed was something I had never seen before. It was a polished black wood platform, much wider than the mattress. It had two steps up, yet the mattress was sunk into the platform, giving off an interesting illusion. The sheets were a soft grey that matched the color of his walls and were tucked in with military precision.

Turning, I scanned over the three bookshelves as I sipped my brady. I never would have picked Eagle to be the type to read, but here before me was proof. Many of them were about leadership, business, and a few biographies. What surprised me was the row of the complete *Harry Potter* series, and from the looks of them, they had been read many times.

"What do you know, Mr. President likes a little fiction in his rigid life."

Getting bored and feeling a buzz kicking in, I wandered back out to the living room and flopped belly-first on the couch. I set my glass and brandy on the coffee table and turned on the TV, flipping through the channels until I landed on a marathon of MTV's *Catfish*. It was trash TV, but I was just tipsy enough to enjoy it. Trying to fill my glass again, I spilled more than made it in my glass, so I gave up and took swigs straight from the bottle. Drunk and lost in my TV show, I had no idea how long I'd been left in the house by myself, so when boots appeared in front of my face, I was surprised.

"Do you know you're watching TV upside down?" Eagle asked me.

"This was the only way I could get the TV to stop moving," I answered, pouting at the frown on his face.

"After drinking that much brandy, I'm amazed you're still able to tell you're watching TV," he replied with a grin on his lips.

I liked kissing those lips. Oh! And his dick. I liked kissing that too. Wonder if he would let me play with it again? Wait, was there a reason that I wasn't going to do that again? Who fucking cares? It was hot and felt amazing, I wanna do it again.

I rolled myself all the way off the couch since my legs were the only thing still on it, the rest of me already on the floor. Kneeling, I looked up at Eagle, who just gave me a questioning look. I crawled up to him and grabbed his jeans to hold myself upright.

"Can I give your dick a mouth hug?" I asked as I rested my head against his crotch.

I heard laughter from behind Eagle, but I couldn't seem to lift my head to see who it could be. Eagle didn't answer me; he just bent down and pulled me up by my armpits. When I was upright, he grabbed my ass and lifted me like a child, wrapping my legs around his waist. I let my arms circle around his neck and nuzzled it, liking the smell of him. It was spicy and wild. The next thing I knew, I was being laid down in a bed and the covers were pulled up around me. After that, the world went dark, and I fell blissfully into sleep.

CHAPTER TWELVE
EAGLE

Looking down at the little hellcat, I couldn't help but smile. She was nothing like any woman I'd ever met before. One moment she was tough as nails, kicking all our asses, then she was passed out in her bed, curled into a ball like a harmless, adorable kitten.

I brushed her soft pink hair out of her face, wanting to see her expression better.

What witchcraft did she use to put me under her spell so fast?

Nothing I did was impulsive. Control was something I craved, needed. When I didn't have it, it caused chaos in me, and that never went well for the people around me. Forcing myself to leave when all I wanted to do was wrap myself around her, I turned and headed back downstairs.

"I'm impressed. If a woman asked me if she could give my dick a mouth hug, I don't think I could have said no and tucked her into bed," Cognac said from the couch.

"That's why I'm president—I can make the tough calls."

He just laughed and turned back to watch his soccer match.

Entering the kitchen, I started to figure out what I wanted to make for dinner. It was a rule in the house that we always had dinner together if we didn't have more pressing matters to attend to. Many of the books and things I'd read showed that sharing a meal built stronger bonds.

"Where did Dax wander off to?" Picasso asked, taking a seat at the counter.

"After consuming almost a full bottle of brandy, I put her to bed where she passed out," I answered as I started washing the ingredients.

I could feel Picasso wanting to say something, but he was holding back. Even though he was my little brother, he never acted like it, always trying to take care of me. Out of the two of us, the club members always went to him with issues first, and he brought it to my attention if he couldn't deal with it. Every leader needed that right-hand man, and Picasso was it for me. We were the perfect team.

"Just say it already," I grumbled.

"Do you really think this can work? You aren't known for sharing things—how can you share a woman with four other people?"

Not wanting to see the look I knew was on his face, I just kept chopping up the vegetables. "Look, I can't explain it, but there is something about her. I can't accept the idea of her leaving."

"Eagle, you haven't even known her a full day. How can you say shit like that?"

Slamming down the knife, I turned to him. "We've been stalking that woman for months. Every one of us knows more about that woman than we do our own mother at this point. Before I even set eyes on her, I knew I needed to meet her, that she was too perfect to let pass out of my life."

"You know this sounds crazy, right? I love you brother, but this is borderline mental."

"I KNOW!" I bellowed at him, glad I no longer had the knife in my hand. Not that I would hurt him, but something would feel my wrath for all the chaos inside me.

Picasso's face hardened as he leaned over the counter and grabbed my shoulders. "You don't get to fucking yell at me, Eagle. We are not like that to each other. Just because I'm telling you truths that you don't want to hear doesn't give you that right. I'm your vice president, your brother, and I'm always in your fucking corner. Always."

I sagged. He was right. "I can't let her go without trying. If it doesn't work, we'll just stick with the original plan, and I promise I will accept it."

"Know that I'll make you keep your word, Eagle," Picasso said, then let go of me and left the kitchen to head to his space in the garage off the side of the house.

Mind full of thoughts, I started working on dinner again, knowing it was the best way to calm myself down. We were going to have enough to feed the whole club, but it was better than me killing someone.

"Hey pres," Sprocket's soft voice said, drawing me back to the present. Seeing he had my attention, he continued. "You were right—she did go through all of our rooms, but we didn't have much to find. Cognac left his notebook, but the information in there, from what I saw, wasn't anything she couldn't have figured out easily with time."

"Do we know where Kimber ran off to?" I asked, not liking that she'd vanished after her meeting with Dax.

"No, but I don't think Two Tricks has her, if that's what

you're worried about. Can't believe that bitch had us thinking she and Dax were tight."

"Dax's brother was a Blackjax, married to the president's daughter, one of the only people to survive Two Tricks' takeover. Guess we all assumed that Dax saved her because she was family," I mused.

Sprocket leaned against the counter, chewing his thumbnail. "What if it was her last act as her being family? Dax could have asked for her to be spared but then disowned her after the fact."

"Sounds reasonable to me. Guess we'll have to wait and see who will tell us the story first," I said with a grin, hoping it would be Kimber so I could show her how wrong it was to fuck with the Phantom Saints.

Chapter Thirteen
Dax

Waking up with a hangover was never something I enjoyed. My head pounded, my tongue stuck to the roof of my mouth, and I felt like I had been run over by a Mack truck. That was the last time I was going to drink a bottle of brandy in the middle of the day. Glancing around, I saw that I was back in the room I first woke up in. *Was it the same day? Or had I slept into the next?*

Carefully, I sat up, letting my feet dangle over the edge of the bed. Looking down, I was just in the t-shirt and my underwear. Someone had taken my shorts off.

"They better not have copped a feel or I'm going to stab someone," I muttered, getting to my feet. I paused, making sure I had my balance before continuing.

The blinds on my window were closed, but I could see the glow of light through the plastic, letting me know it wasn't night. I shuffled my way to the bathroom, forgetting to knock before shoving the door open.

"Well, look who it is," Sprocket said with a grin. He was

standing at the sink completely naked, looking at me through the mirror.

Not having the energy to deal with him, I started the shower and stripped out of the few clothes I had left. Checking the water was hot, I hopped in and let the spray rush over my skin, helping with the muscle ache.

Seconds later, Sprocket was in the shower with me. I glared at him but knew it lacked any power behind it. My brain just hurt too much to give two shits. Squirting shampoo into my hand, I mushed it on my hair and carelessly scrubbed. Hands stilled mine and pulled them from my scalp. When they were at my sides, Sprocket started to massage my aching skull with his strong fingers.

"Oh god," I moaned and relaxed into his touch.

He let his fingers drift down to my neck and worked on some of the tension there as well. I leaned my head forward, giving him better access, and let my body go slack against his. I could feel his dick wedged between my ass cheeks, but he didn't make any move to draw attention to it. Grasping my shoulders, he turned me around and helped the water rinse out the soap. When he started the process all over again with the conditioner, I wanted to purr with how content I was.

Never in my whole life had I let someone wash my hair unless they were cutting it. This felt so decadent that I didn't know how I'd ever be able to do it myself again. When he washed out the conditioner, he moved to take the washcloth and soaped it up. Methodically, he scrubbed my skin with firm movements that were more purposeful than sexual. The feeling of being so cared for was new for me—other than Wes and Devin, no one had ever given two shits about me. My various foster parents saw me as a check in the mail, and the other kids just saw me as competition for attention.

When Sprocket was done, I turned to repay the favor, but instead he picked me up, set me outside the tub, wrapped me in a towel, and stepped back to finish his own shower. I stood there, stunned, watching the shower curtain Sprocket had disappeared behind.

Did he not want me? From the rock-hard dick, I knew he liked me enough to want to fuck me. Why would he do something like that without wanting something in return?

Cocking my head to the side, I waited just in case he changed his mind and reached out to grab me, but he never did. Totally confused, I grabbed my clothes off the floor and headed back to my room. I took my time to towel off, still trying to process the fact that Sprocket, a stranger, had just taken the time to care for me.

Whatever it was that Sprocket did made me feel human again. Pulling on the shorts from yesterday, I grabbed a tank top that was tie-dyed. It was long and baggy, so I had to knot one side of it so I didn't look like I was wearing a ridiculously short dress. Giving my hair a good finger comb, I was as ready as I was going to be to face another day in captivity.

"I should start a journal," I mused to myself as I wandered down to the kitchen. "All the cool people in history kept a written log of their life in imprisonment."

I still had no idea what time it was, but seeing Void, Cognac, and Picasso all sitting at the counter eating gave me a clue that it was too early for me. They all looked up from their food as if shocked to see me standing there.

Picasso twisted on the stool to look at me. "Um, Dax, do you know what time it is?"

"Your question is making me scared to ask," I said,

refusing to glance at any surface that told time. "Is there any coffee made before I hear the bad news?"

Void pushed himself up and headed into the kitchen. I watched as he pulled a mug down and left it by the half-full coffee pot. Guessing it was for me, I wandered over and filled the cup to the brim, then took a large gulp of the smooth, dark, nectar of the gods. As the coffee made its way into my system, I just stood, resting against the counter until it worked its magic. When I opened them again, I found all three guys watching me with varying expressions of lust.

"What?" I snapped, not liking the how predatory they all looked.

Cognac gave me a slow smile full of unfulfilled promises. "You *really* like coffee."

I frowned, not understanding why he would say it like that. "Everyone likes coffee—it makes the earth spin, the sun rise, and the general population function without killing too many people."

"All I know is I don't moan like that when I drink my first cup of coffee. You, on the other hand, sounded like you might have just orgasmed," Void said, resting his chin on his hand as he watched me.

Eagle walked into the kitchen, taking in the whole scene, and smiled. "No, when she orgasms it sounds *way* better than that."

My mouth fell open at the casual way Eagle was talking about the spontaneous, angry sex we had. *What the fuck was going on right now?* Something had definitely changed from yesterday to today. I needed to know what it was, and fast.

Thankfully, no one seemed to want to comment, so I let it drop, worried what other ridiculous shit would be said.

Halfway done with my first cup, I turned and topped it off, then I caught the time on the coffeemaker.

"What the bitch-tits am I doing up at seven a.m.?!" I yelled, whirling to turn on the guys as if they were to blame. "I already took a shower, so that means I was awake when I typically go to bed!"

Eagle, unbothered by my outburst, grabbed his own coffee mug and walked over to fill it. When I didn't move out of his way, he boxed me in, pressing up against me as he poured his brew. Leaning back, he kissed me on the forehead and backed up a step to lean against the island. Horny and handsy I could handle, but *that*—that whole sweet routine thing—was freaking me out.

"Do you know what time you passed out and went to bed?" he asked with a smirk.

Glaring at him, I scrunched up my face. "You drink that much brandy and tell me if you could remember that kind of shit."

"Some of us can handle our liquor better than others," Cognac piped up, adding in his opinion.

"Fuck you. I'm half your weight, you asshole. Of course you can drink more than I can," I grumbled. "Normally I can outdrink most people, but I didn't have anything to eat."

Cognac cupped a hand around his ear. "I'm sorry, all I hear are excuses. Let me know when the real talk is coming."

I lunged for him, but Eagle caught my arm and pulled me against him, wrapping his arms around me. Effectively trapped, I huffed and wriggled, trying to get him to let me go.

"If you keep rubbing your ass on my dick, I'm going to take it as a sign that you want me to fuck you right here, right now," Eagle whispered in my ear.

I froze, my body and mind at war with each other. My body begged for him to do that very thing and let the others watch, while my brain screamed for me to run away. Going for middle ground, I stopped fighting him and just relaxed, letting him hold me.

"I would guess since you slept close to thirteen hours, your body didn't need to sleep anymore. If I went to bed at five o'clock, I would be up at six-thirty too," Eagle said, shifting so he held me around my waist, freeing my arms.

I looked up at him, surprised. "I passed out at five?!"

He grinned down at me. "We got back from work, and there you were, laying upside-down, falling off the couch, drunk off your ass watching TV. Can't say I've watched *Catfish* before, but you really seemed to be into it if the way you were screaming at the people was any clue."

Covering my face with my hands, I groaned. "God, did I do anything else embarrassing?"

Please don't tell me I was wasted enough for them to ask me questions about Two Tricks. I knew better than to get that drunk. I never remembered what I said.

Looking up at the guys, I could tell there was something else I did that was noteworthy.

"I think my favorite part was when you asked if you could give Eagle's dick a mouth hug," Void said, smiling at me.

"Fucking Harper and her Urban Dictionary addiction. Why does she teach me all those stupid phrases?" I said, going limp against Eagle and looking back up at him. "My bad. Didn't mean to get your hopes up that was ever gonna happen again."

Wait, why was I apologizing to him? What the fuck did I care? I should have welcomed the chance to puke all over him if he tried to shove his dick down my throat.

"Oh, is that right? Never going to happen again? I highly doubt that, little hellcat. In the meantime, we'll just have to make sure you're not left to your own devices for that long. That was a two-hundred-dollar bottle of brandy. If you keep drinking like that, you'll be a very expensive houseguest." Eagle let me go and pushed me towards the other guys. "Sit down and I'll make you my hangover special."

Snagging my coffee, I cautiously made my way over to the other three. When they didn't scatter even though they were clearly finished with all their food, I took the seat they pulled out for me between Void and Picasso. I couldn't place why I was so wary of them all this morning. They hadn't done anything aggressive to me, but that was exactly what was wrong.

They were no longer acting like I was a prisoner they didn't trust or want in their house. Yesterday I'd been left with just one of them or on my own to keep myself entertained. Now they all seemed more intent on being around me.

Did they find out information that I don't know about? Did Wes make contact, trying to get me back by pretending to be Two Tricks? It wouldn't be the first time he'd done that.

I still couldn't figure it out, and it was driving me crazy. I needed to scout out who would be the easiest to break and try and get them alone to pump them for information.

"All of us have work we need to get done, but I'll have one of the guys around all day," Eagle said as he moved around the kitchen. "I also thought it might be good for you to meet some of the old ladies in the club. Figured it might be better for one of them to go shopping for the things you need."

"Any chance I can go with them?" I dared to ask. Eagle's furrowed brow gave me my answer. "Was worth a shot," I said, shrugging my shoulders.

"Just in case you forgot, each of us have an app on our phones that lets us control the ankle monitor you have on. So if you get too far from one of us or try and take them out, the other four of us can zap your ass just as easily from wherever we are," Eagle reminded me with a wink as he set a plate of food down in front of me. "Just making sure things are clear between us all."

Looking down at what he made me, my stomach growled, excited to taste this magical combination of food. Scrambled eggs, bacon, and cheese between two toasted waffles covered in syrup. Half of me wanted to grab it and shove it into my mouth, but I decided that would be an insult to this creation. Picking up the knife and fork, I dove into the meal, humming happily and bouncing in my seat. Each bite was bliss.

"Picasso was right, food definitely puts you in a good mood." Eagle chuckled as he started working on his own waffle sandwich without the syrup.

Mouth full of the delightful meal, I ignored his comment. I paused my chewing when Sprocket joined us in the kitchen, making himself a cup of hot tea. For some reason, this piqued my interest. Not that there was anything wrong with not liking coffee, I just didn't picture him as that guy.

"You'll spend the morning with Sprocket; the rest of us have things to do off the compound," Eagle said, pulling my attention back to him. "One of us should be back later this afternoon to relieve him of your company."

Resting my chin on my hand, I batted my lashes. "Don't

hurry home on my account. I'm sure I can find some way to amuse myself."

"That's what we're worried about," Picasso grumbled.

Shoving the last part of his breakfast into his mouth, Eagle rinsed off his plate and loaded it into the dishwasher. *I wonder how much it would bother him if I left my dishes in the sink?* I chuckled, picturing his eye twitching and him trying to hold back from strangling me.

Lost in my own imagination, I startled when hands grabbed my hips and spun me around on the stool. Eagle looked down at me, his eyes full of possessiveness. He grabbed my chin in one large hand, tilting my head back as he gave me a brutal kiss. Shocked, I didn't respond right away, but as he nipped at my lips, I couldn't help but rise to the challenge and open up to him.

When he pulled back, there was a satisfied grin on his lips, which were red from our kiss. "See you soon, little hellcat."

He signaled to the rest of the guys, and all but Sprocket followed after him, totally unfazed by the makeout session we had right in front of them. It didn't bother me—I wasn't shy—but that kiss seemed to mean something to the others.

Chapter Fourteen
Sprocket

I could see the wheels turning in Dax's brain, taking in everything that had just happened.

We all knew what Eagle had done. Now the gloves were off, and she was fair game. Knowing that I had the whole morning alone with her made me smile. I was going to take her apart piece by piece until I could figure her out, see what made her tick.

Being the quiet guy allowed me to observe people, watch them when they didn't notice I was in the room. It gave me an advantage as an adult, but it was born from years of abuse and self-preservation. From the little time I'd spent watching Dax, I could tell she had a kindred spirit. She'd been through her own version of hell and fought to land on top. My fingers itched to peel back the layers of sass and bravado to see what was really hidden at her core.

"You can take a picture if you want, that way you can stare at it whenever you like," Dax said, glancing at me from the corner of her eye.

I shook my head slowly. "Pictures never do the real thing justice."

Dax snorted as she turned to give me her full attention. Her silver-blue eyes wandered over me, searching for anything she could use to figure me out. I knew what happened between us this morning had caught her off guard and she still couldn't decide what to make of it. Grinning, I gulped down the last of my tea before grabbing her plate and putting it in the dishwasher.

"Well, babysitter, what's on the agenda?" Dax asked, trying to get a rise out of me.

"I have work to do in the shop. Parts came in yesterday so I can finish up a few bikes," I answered, walking to the pool table and grabbing the pair of black lace-up combat boots off them. "Here—you're going to need these. Can't let you hang around wearing flip-flops."

She took them from me and looked at the size, her eyes widening. "How did you know my size?"

"It's a talent, I guess you could say. I've always been good at matching up parts," I said, giving her a wink. I liked seeing her off balance; she was far too used to being in control, and I wasn't going to make it that easy. "Come on, we're burning daylight."

"Fuck that. The daylight only showed up an hour ago, it can give me a minute," Dax grumbled as she pulled out the pair of socks I had stuffed in one boot.

Muttering to herself, she pulled on both boots but could only lace one up halfway because of the ankle tracker. Finished, she clomped her way over to me and stopped with her hands on her hips, eyes bright with irritation. "Well, let's get on with it."

Today was going to be a fun day.

Chapter Fifteen
Dax

"Hell no, I am not sitting on this stool and watching you work all morning," I grumbled when Sprocket presented me with my perch. "I'll have you know that I'm very mechanical."

Sprocket leaned against his workbench with his arms crossed, watching me with those intelligent green eyes. I'd met a lot of people in my line of work, and it was the ones with eyes like his that scared me the most. They seemed to be able to look into your soul and make you spill all your secrets.

Not this girl—I had too much at stake to let a handsome face with hands that could do the Lord's work get anything out of me.

"I'll be the judge of that. Why don't we start you out with being my tool runner and go from there," Sprocket said, pushing off from the bench and gesturing to the rows of tool drawers behind him. "Feel free to look through them and familiarize yourself with where things are."

Rolling my eyes, I pulled open the closest drawer and saw it filled with sockets of all sizes, along with various wrench handles in different lengths. I had to admit as I worked my way through the bench that he had an amazing collection of high-end equipment. Peeking over my shoulder, I saw him standing at the hydraulic worktable with the motorcycle he was working on, unboxing parts.

"One might think that with so many tools you might be compensating for something." I smirked as I looked at the drawer with the impact wrenches in it, hefting one up for show.

Sprocket set down the box and gave me a disapproving look. "Now Dax, I'm pretty sure you know that's not true. You know exactly what I'm working with—or did my cock rubbing on your pert little ass slip your mind?"

The shock of hearing him talk so bluntly caught me off guard. I could not seem to get a read on this guy. One minute he was sweet and soft-spoken, then he pulled shit like this. As he held my gaze, he walked over to me and pulled me flush against his chest, making sure to pin my pelvis to his. In this position, there was no way that I could miss the size of the equipment he was packing in his jeans.

"In case you needed a reminder," Sprocket said, nipping at my earlobe before releasing me. "Now, if you could grab me a half-inch socket wrench, that would be lovely."

Gulping as he turned back to the bike, I shook myself out of my lust-filled stupor and grabbed what he asked for.

After that incident, I decided that he was too dangerous to tease casually, so I kept silent as I observed the comings and goings of the shop. There were four other men that worked there, but none of them really interacted with us. They seemed content to shit-talk each other and leave Sprocket to his work. Outside the garage, I saw women chatting as they headed off in cars, presumably to do shopping or whatever else off the compound lands. Other members came and went on bikes or headed into the clubhouse.

What surprised me the most was that everyone seemed very content to be here. The women looked happy, and none of them seemed worried about the rough-looking men hanging around. I didn't see said men getting sloppy drunk by noon and harassing the women or causing fights like I'd always imagined. For the most part, this seemed like any other cul-de-sac with people who actually liked spending time with their neighbors.

"What do you say about taking a lunch break?" Sprocket said, pulling me out of my musings.

Glancing up at the clock, I was shocked to see that it was indeed noon. "Sure, I'm always up for food."

Sprocket grinned at that. "I'll bet you are. Word on the street is that food is your weakness."

"There is nothing wrong with liking to eat. Try growing up unsure if you're going to get one meal, let alone three, in a day," I growled, frowning at him.

"Hmm, so I'm guessing you didn't have the 'white picket fence' childhood," he said as he wiped off his hands on a rag.

I stiffened, not really wanting to delve into my childhood. No one but Wes knew my whole story, and that suited me just fine. "Let's go with 'I never had a chance to wear rose-colored glasses.'"

Sprocket watched me for a moment before turning to head out of the garage, apparently assuming I was going to follow him. Groaning, I stomped a foot and headed after him back to the house.

"Make sure you take your boots off or Eagle will beat your ass, and not in a fun way," Sprocket warned.

"God, if he and Wes ever meet, I think they might be best friends. Or kill each other," I muttered, kicking off my boots and letting them fall where they will. "Wes can't stand a messy house either—that's why I have my own floor, so I can be as messy as I please."

"Wes... you mean your business partner Weston?" Sprocket asked as he pulled out what looked like items to make a sandwich from the fridge.

"Figured you guys would have known about him if you're any good at your research," I said, hopping up on a stool.

Sprocket paused in making his food to look up with me mischief in his eyes. "We found you, didn't we? I would say that alone speaks for our skills."

"It was only a matter of time until someone gave me up if you paid enough or threatened them the right way. The downside of my job is you can't trust anyone to watch your back," I said, shrugging my shoulders.

"Yet you trust Weston." It was more a statement than a question.

"Hmm, well, he is different," I said. "Weston is my family. He and I have been through hell and back. Much like I would guess you and the other four guys."

"Aren't we lucky people to find something like that in our lives?" Sprocket mused as he picked up his plate and sat down at the counter next to me.

I couldn't help but grin at the fact that this asshole was making a statement when he didn't make me a sandwich. Both Eagle and Picasso had made me all of my meals since I had been here, but Sprocket was not planning on catering to me.

Hopping off my stool, I wandered over and made my sandwich. Making sure to pile it full of as much meat and cheese as I could, I added one leaf of lettuce, knowing Wes would have yelled if I didn't eat enough vegetables. After slathering the bread with mayo, I put it all together and cut it corner to corner, then added some BBQ chips to my plate. Pulling open the fridge and grabbing a can of Mountain Dew, I took my meal back to my seat, pleased with myself.

"I think you forgot something, princess," Sprocket said with a grin on his face, eyes full of humor.

I frowned, looking down at the feast in front of me, then back to him. "What?"

"That last person always cleans up," Sprocket instructed.

"How do we *know* I'm the last person? The other guys could come back and want to make a sandwich."

Sprocket just shook his head. "They are off the property until later today. I got a text an hour or so ago that they ran into a little trouble, so I get to hang with you for a few more minutes until Tilly is free."

"Fine. I'll put it all away when I'm done," I huffed.

Sprocket grabbed my plate and slid it away from me. "Nope, not gonna work. If you wait too long in this heat, you could make the meat or the cheese go bad." Before I could control my face, my lower lip popped out in a pout as he blocked me from my meal. "The longer you take pouting, the longer it will be before you get to eat."

I growled at him as I went back to the kitchen and started to put things away. "If you touch one chip on my plate, I'm going to stab you with a rusty fork!"

Sprocket's eyebrows shot up at my words. "My, that is a very specific threat. I have to know—do you have a rusty fork hidden somewhere on you?" he asked as he poked at a chip on the top of my pile.

I grabbed the knife I used for the mayo and threw it at

Sprocket, letting it hit the wooden countertop right next to his hand. "Fresh out of rusty forks at the moment, but I do have plenty of knives around."

Sprocket didn't even blink as he removed the knife from the counter and gave me an impressed look. "That's quite an arm on you. Not many people could get a butter knife to stick in such thick wood."

What the hell would it take to freak this guy out? Didn't he realize that I could have killed him? Or at least really stabbed him with that knife?

Trying not to show how much he threw me off my game, I put the last of the food away and came back to my seat. Sprocket slid my plate over, and I dove in, ignoring his chuckles as I glared at him.

"Hello!" a female voice called out from the front door.

Sprocket stood and opened the door, letting in a woman who gave him a wide smile, which he returned. For some reason I couldn't even begin to explain, I did NOT like this woman looking at Sprocket like that.

"Tilly, welcome. Thank you for looking out for Dax today. It seems that they lost all her belongings at the airport, so I scrounged up what I could," Sprocket said, lying through his teeth.

Tilly was beautiful. Tall with thick, long, brunette hair that had that effortless wave girls killed for. Her slim body was accented by her tight ripped jeans and t-shirt that said *Real Women Ride,* which was cut into a crop top. Turning, she finally took me in with warm brown eyes that seemed friendly.

"Oh god, please don't tell me that they have been forcing you to wear shit like that?" Tilly said with a wrinkled nose and wide eyes.

Okay, I kind of liked her.

"Not the worst I've had to make do with," I said, shrugging my shoulders.

"Come on, babes," Tilly said, waving me over. "We'll get you sorted out, and tomorrow I'll go out and get you some real clothes."

I grabbed my plate since I wasn't done with my food and hopped off the stool.

"Dax... leave the plate here," Sprocket said, frowning down at me.

I looked down at my half-eaten meal, then back at him. "Nope," I said, popping the P. "I'm gonna take it with me. Don't worry, I'll bring it back."

Sprocket tried to lunge at me to grab the plate, but I skipped out of his way and growled at him, practically baring my teeth. "Don't touch my fucking food, asshat. You try it again and I can't guarantee you will keep all your fingers."

"Yup, we are going to be good friends, Dax. Come on, let's hang out at my house," Tilly said, grinning at the scene unfolding before her.

"Be good, Dax!" Sprocket called out as we walked out.

"In your dreams, douchecanoe!" I yelled back.

Tilly almost fell down the stairs, she was laughing so hard. "Girl, you must have balls of steel to talk to him that way. Do you treat all of them like that?"

"I give what I get. So sue me," I said, glaring over my shoulder at the house. "If they didn't act like such cavemen, then I wouldn't have to beat into their heads how to treat a woman."

"Preach it girl! It took me years to whip my men into shape. He still needs a reminder every so often, but the make-up sex is so worth it," Tilly shared as I followed her further in the surrounding houses behind Eagle's.

All of them were simple one- or two-story homes that looked like the premanufactured type that you buy and just have placed on the land. Tilly walked up to a cute ranch-style house with brick walls in cream and gray coloring. It had a small front porch with a swing on it that looked well used. Opening the front door, she led me into a living room that was warm and inviting.

Tilly flopped down on one of the overstuffed cream-colored couches and waved for me to join her. "Make yourself at home, Mutt won't be back until late. He's working at the shop near L.A."

"*Mutt?* Is that your husband?" I asked, noticing the rings on her left hand.

"Yeah, that dipshit is mine," Tilly said, laughing. "After six years, I guess I'll claim him."

"Wow, you guys have been married for six years?" I was impressed.

"No, we have been married for two years, but together for six. Gator—my other husband—and I have been together since we were ten. He's out of town right now. He does recon work for Eagle on new business prospects," Tilly said casually, as if she hadn't just told me she had two husbands.

I opened my mouth to say something, but everything I wanted to ask would make me sound like an asshole.

"It's fine, ask away. I'm used to it after all these years," Tilly said, smirking at me.

"So... You have two husbands," I confirmed, figuring that would be a safe place to start.

Tilly bounced out of the couch and walked over to grab a picture off a bookshelf. It was of Tilly in a wedding dress, two handsome men in tuxes standing on either side of her. They all looked so happy together, I couldn't help but be jealous.

That would never happen for me. It was too dangerous to let someone get involved in my life that way.

"You look beautiful, Tilly, and not bad choices in the male department, if you don't mind me saying," I commented, handing her back the picture.

"They are idiots at times, but we really are very happy," Tilly said, gazing down at the picture with love in her eyes. "I never would have thought it would work out this way, but I can't imagine my life without both of them in it. No way could I have ever chosen between the two of them. I loved them both, and they felt the same about me, so we said 'to hell with it' and did what we really wanted, even if it isn't the norm."

"That is amazing. I hope that everyone can find happiness like you guys have. Too many people are worried about what people think and give up what they really want."

"Girl, I couldn't have said it better. Who knows—you might even end up with a man or two—or five—yourself," Tilly giggled.

"Wait, what?! No, I don't think so. Those boys are not interested in a relationship with me. We hardly know each other. Besides, I know what they want from me, and I don't think I'll ever be able to give it to them," I said, frowning down at my ankle.

"Look, I know the story they are telling people is bullshit, so why don't you fill me in on what's really going on. I might be able to help." Tilly curled up with a pillow, looking at me with wide, innocent eyes.

I snorted. "As wonderful as that sounds, I doubt you would turn on your fellow 'family' members here at the MC."

At my words, Tilly's face sobered. "What are those fuckers up to? Are you in trouble? Are they holding you against your will? I will not stand for that shit happening in this family!"

"You have anything to drink? I think we're gonna need it for this story," I said, seeing the genuine anger in her eyes at what might be happening to me.

"Give me a sec," Tilly said, heading into the kitchen. "How do we feel about wine? Otherwise I have some tequila!"

My stomach rolled at the sound of tequila after my adventures last night. "I think wine might be the safer option."

Tilly returned to the living room, handing me a glass of wine and setting the bottle on the table before she settled back into the couch. "Okay, hit me."

Taking a deep breath and a swig of wine, I started with the meeting at my shop. Watching her face as I told my story was better than I'd hoped. If this went as planned, I might have my inside person. She had been with this club for so long, she knew everyone and definitely had information that could help me.

Shocking me, she grabbed my leg and yanked it into her lap to see the tracker.

"I'm going to kill that fucking rat bastard when I see him next. You can't just fucking kidnap a woman so she does what you want! What, did he watch 365 *Days* one too many times?!" Tilly fumed as she stood and paced the living room. "So they are doing this so that you give up all the information you know about your boss? They've come up with some idiotic ideas before, but this one really puts the icing on the cake."

"Would you be willing to help me reach out to someone? I just need them to know that I'm okay and where I am so they can come get me," I said, daring to hope she would let me reach out to Wes.

Tilly turned and looked at me, hands on her hips like she was a mother bear and I was her cub. "You bet your ass I'll help you. Why the hell they thought holding anyone hostage was a good idea, I will never know."

"Do you have a cell phone I can use?" I asked, my heart fluttering with the hope I might be getting out of this place.

Tilly pulled her phone out of her back pocket and handed it over to me. I typed in Wes's number and sent him a text with the codeword that would let him know that it was me before deleting the text and calling him.

He answered on the first ring. "Dax, what the fuck?! How could you have gone silent after sending me a message like that?"

"Fuck you, Weston," I snapped, not liking the panic that'd been in his voice. "You have no idea what's going on. It took me until now to get a phone so I could reach out to you. The motherfuckers have a tracking anklet on me that they rigged to shock me if I try to escape."

I stood and walked to the window, trying to have some kind of privacy without making Tilly feel like she was being used.

"Tell me what I need to know so I can get you out of there. What is the model of the anklet?" Wes asked, turning all business.

Setting my foot on the closest chair, I looked all over the band but couldn't see any markings to tell me anything. "There is nothing helpful on the outside of the band, but I'll describe it best I can. It's waterproof, two inches wide and about half an inch thick. I don't see any plug-in ports, so I'm guessing it's bluetooth or wirelessly programmed. They said the shock feature was added aftermarket, so there has to be someone we know who can find the people who do that. Seems like it'd be a small market to me."

I could hear Wes typing away as I talked, grunting his answers. "What can you tell me about where you are? The signal on all your devices was cut off before I could get the final location."

"They have lots of land, an old cattle farm of some kind. It's a whole compound with twenty homes, a barn turned clubhouse, and a mechanic shop. If you get any aerial photos, it shouldn't be hard to find," I said, rattling off all that I could think of that might help him.

"Hold tight, Dax. I'm coming for you. I promise I'll get you out of there," Wes said. The anger in his voice made me shiver, glad he was on my side.

"I trust you, Wes—"

I was abruptly cut off when a hand wrapped around my neck, and I let out a squeak as the phone was yanked out of my hand.

"Who is this?" Void's deep voice demanded.

Chapter Sixteen
Dax

I could hear Wes's muffled response but couldn't make out the words he said to Void.

Void let out a harsh laugh as his eyes glanced down to me, danger flickering in them. "Listen, you can give all the threats you want, but our little demon isn't going anywhere."

Now I could hear Weston yelling into the phone, making Void smirk as his grip on my neck tightened.

"Sounds like fun. Can't wait to meet you if you decide to act on your threats," Void said before he hung up and pocketed the phone.

"Just you fucking wait until he gets here," I snarled as I tried to wriggle out of his hold. "Trust me, Weston isn't someone to mess with."

Void just grunted and nodded to Tilly. "I'll get you your phone back to you as soon as we know she didn't do anything else to it."

"Void, you've always been a bastard, but this is a new

low, even for you," Tilly snapped, frowning with her arms crossed over her chest.

"Don't ask for trouble, Tilly. This isn't a matter you want to get involved in. Tell Mutt I said hey," he added as he dragged me out of the house.

Once we were out on the road, I made my move, kicking out his left knee. He loosened his grip, needing both his hands so he didn't eat dirt. Knowing I couldn't run, I decided to just take out my frustration on him instead. I leaped onto his back and put him in a chokehold, wrapping my legs around his middle. I squeezed my arm around his neck as tight as I could as he rolled us over so he was laying on top of me, pressing me into the ground. He reached back and grabbed a handful of my hair and pulled, making me hiss in pain.

"That's a fucking chick move, dickface," I growled.

Rolling once more so we were both on our sides, I felt him rummaging in his pocket for something. Then when I saw his phone, I released him and shoved away so I could spring to my feet. I wasn't going to let that bastard taser me because I got the drop on him. Lunging over him, I grabbed for his phone and knocked it out of his hands, but he grabbed my legs and flipped me back. The thud my body made slamming into the dirt would have made any wrestler proud. Any air that I had in my lungs came whooshing out, leaving me stunned for a moment. Void loomed over me with a wicked grin on his face, his icy blue eyes alight with the challenge.

"Chick move or not, it always does the trick," Void wheezed. "Seems like our little demon is upset about something? I'll play, let's see what you got."

Letting out a snarl, I rolled so I could get to my feet and faced off with Void. I tilted my neck side to side, checking to see how hard I hit, but it wasn't the worst I'd experienced. Seeing Void's stance made me think of the MMA poster that he had in his room. I gave him a knowing grin that seemed to make him curious—I had the upper hand now that I knew what type of fighting he was trained in.

"Let's make this more interesting. If I win, then I get to go free," I said, raising a challenging brow at him.

"Ah, little demon, you know I can't do that. Ask for something else," Void countered.

"Fine. Then I get to go shopping for my own clothes and you assholes have to pay for it all," I said, knowing they had no idea. Even if I didn't usually choose to buy designer clothes, my best friend had taught me well.

"That I can work with. Now, if I win, you have to stay with us for a month without trying to escape," Void said, shocking the shit out of me.

"What happens after that month?" I asked, knowing that they could be planning on killing me if I wouldn't give them what they wanted or if Tricks never came for me.

Void just shrugged. "Who knows, but I can guarantee that during that month you will be treated like a guest and be well provided for. You will be free to roam where you like on the compound, but the tracker stays."

"Fuck it. Not like I'm gonna lose anyway," I said, shrugging my shoulders. "Any rules?"

"Such confidence, little demon. I like it." Void gave me a smile that was mostly teeth. "No rules. Give me all you got."

No rules—what a rookie mistake. If there was one thing I excelled in with hand-to-hand, it was fighting dirty.

Void and I faced off, crouching as I bounced on the balls of my bare feet, having kicked off my flip flops. I could see that he favored Muay Thai as he placed his right leg forward with his weight on his left, ready to strike. Being small, I needed to move faster, and Kung Fu was more my jam. Void struck first, leaping forward with his knee and left fist. I ducked under his punch and grabbed his ankle, pulling it out straight and knocking him off balance. He tumbled to the ground and rolled so he could hop up on his feet.

Curling in, he fell more into a boxing stance, watching me as I circled him. Watching his body for any sign that he was going to attack, I made my move. Darting forward, I kicked out low, then jumped and aimed a shot at his head. Moving faster than I thought he could, his hand snapped out and grabbed my ankle, tossing me away from him. Thudding to the ground, I skidded, just missing getting slammed into a tree.

"You must have a death wish, Void," I threatened as my anger grew.

As I got to my feet, I grabbed a handful of dirt and charged straight for Void's chest. Twisting to slide between his legs, I flung the dirt into his eyes and kneed his balls as I went through. Void roared but kicked out behind him, catching me on the cheek, making my eyes blur. Scrabbling, I tried to get to my feet, but Void was on me, wrapping me up in some crazy Jiu Jitsu hold that no matter how I moved I couldn't get free from. I didn't have the body strength to win at wrestling.

Rolling so I was looking up at the setting sun, Void's chest was heaving under me, letting me know I hadn't made this easy on him. I wriggled around, not willing to give up just yet. Void let out a groan, but it had nothing to do with pain and all to do with his dick hardening under my ass.

"Little demon, I will fuck you up against a tree in front of everyone, or you could admit your defeat," Void growled in my ear, sending shivers through my body.

Making his point further, he plucked at one of my nipples and let his teeth run along the shell of my ear.

"What is it with you guys going all caveman on me when I fight back?" I grumbled, remembering how Eagle ended up fucking me against the bathroom counter.

"Might have something to do with this sexy little demon who feels the need to fight us on everything. Not many people would dare pick a fight with the leaders of the Phantom Saints," Void said as he started to nip down my neck and take my breast in hand.

As much as I wanted to fight him, I couldn't when all I wanted to do was beg him not to stop. I arched into his hands, demanding more from them as I let out a whimper. The moment Void felt the fight drain out of me, he let me go and got to his feet.

Surprised by the change in mood, I wasn't prepared when he grabbed me and tossed me over his shoulder.

"Do I even want to ask?" a strange male asked.

Void just laughed and patted my ass. "Nothing all that interesting. Just picking up our little demon from hanging out with Tilly."

"Oh, is this the famous woman who has been wreaking havoc amongst the leadership?" The man chuckled.

I pushed up, trying to get a glimpse of who Void was talking to, but a sharp smack to my ass had me flopping against his back. "She would be the one. I apologize if anything she said to Tilly got her upset, but she needs to know that we are doing what is best for the club and that she should keep her opinion to herself."

The man groaned. "Great! Thanks for letting your hellion get my old lady all heated. Do you have any idea how long it's going to take me to calm her down, if I even can? Gator is so much better at dealing with that side of her."

"Sorry Mutt, we thought that having her make friends would settle her down a bit. Seems that might have backfired." Void shifted me as I started to wriggle off his shoulder.

"Void, you better not be telling my husband that we can't be friends! I expect to be able to spend some quality bonding time with that woman you have tossed over your shoulder like a sack of potatoes," Tilly called from her porch, hand on her hips.

"Please don't make this harder on me," Mutt whispered to Void.

"If she keeps to her end of the deal, then there shouldn't be any problem with you ladies spending time together," Void said to Tilly over his shoulder.

Tilly just harrumphed and turned on her heel, slamming her front door.

"Wish me luck—I'm going in," Mutt said with a sigh.

"If you need a drink, our door is always open." Void clapped him on the back, and we headed off.

I let the silence hang between us as I decided what my next move was going to be. I had lost the fight. Did I really intend to hold my end of the deal up? Could I volunteer to stay here for a month?

Why the hell was I even thinking this was a possibility? I had a business to run and asses to beat. There was shit going on in the Hidden Empire, and I needed to be there to do my part.

"Did I break you? You're awfully quiet," Void said, jostling me with his shoulder.

"What did dear Weston say to you on the phone?" I asked, curious if he would even tell me.

"Did you teach him how to threaten people or is he that creative on his own?" Void mused as he set me down on the first step of the porch.

I raised a brow at Void as he kept his hands on my hips. "I would say that I started his education, but he took it to heart and really learned the finer aspects of dishing out threats."

Void raised a hand and let his thumb brush over the cheek that he kicked with his biker boot. It hadn't bothered me, but now that he'd reminded me about it, I could feel how swollen it was getting.

"Swelling isn't too bad, but you're going to have one hell of a bruise," he said, caressing my jawline as he dropped his hand.

"Damn, Void, you're about to be in major trouble when Eagle sees that," Cognac said, appearing in the front yard.

Void just grunted and headed up the steps, leaving me with the smiling wet dream—literally. He was in swim trunks, and his skin was still wet and glistening in the fading sunlight. He took his towel and wiped off his face before throwing it over a shoulder, but that still left his bronze abs for me to gawk at.

"Careful. You're starting to drool, *loba*," Cognac said, leaning in close as he passed me. "Come on, dinner should be about ready."

"Where is there a POOL?!" I finally managed to ask once he wasn't in my direct line of sight.

Cognac turned and lifted a finger to his full lips. "It's a secret. We only tell a select few people about our hidden oasis."

"You mean the compounds pool behind the garage?" Sprocket said, wrapping an arm around my waist and herding me up the last few steps. "Don't believe a word this idiot says, there is a huge inground pool just out back. Once we get you something you can swim in, you can check it out for yourself."

"Oh, so you just want to see me in an itty-bitty bikini, hmm?" I taunted.

Sprocket paused and frowned down at me. "On second thought, shorts and a t-shirt would be better."

My brows shot up as I gave him a wide-eyed look. "Seriously?"

Sprocket leaned in until I could feel the heat of his breath along my neck. "No one but us gets to see your delectable little body."

Frozen in place, I watched him disappear into the house. "What the fuck is going on?"

Chapter Seventeen
Weston

After getting hung up on by whichever of the biker trash that was holding Dax, I chucked my phone against the wall. It shattered, flying into a million pieces as I let out a roar of anger. I paced back and forth in my office, which was filled with all the equipment I used to monitor the Hidden Empire, knowing it wouldn't do me any damn good to get Dax back. I knew where she was and who was holding her, but I couldn't find a way to get her out without starting an all-out war with one of the biggest biker gangs on the West Coast.

I ran over our brief conversation again, trying to see if she had left me any more clues to get her out. Together we had made backup plans for almost any scenario, but the Phantom Saints had played on my cockiness. Never once had I thought I would let her get taken—it was my job to keep her safe and watch her back.

They put a fucking shock collar on her!

The sound of my second cell went off, letting me know

it was something to do with Empire business. Only Dax had the number to the cell I destroyed.

"What," I snapped. There was a pause on the line before they spoke.

"Wes, we can't get ahold of Dax, and we got a big problem." It was Brian, one of Dax's men.

"Are you going to tell me what the problem is, or do I have to guess?" I asked, unable to hold back my irritation.

Out of the two of us, Dax was the volatile one. I kept my cool for the both of us, but having her taken from me was proving to be my undoing.

"Right. Sorry, Wes. It seems that the De León cartel is claiming that Dax killed their son while he was in L.A. on vacation. They're saying that if we don't hand her over, they will make moves against us."

"How the fuck am I just hearing about this now?!" I yelled into the phone. "This is not the sort of thing that we should be blindsided with."

"I just found out myself. Dax was my first call, but her phone went right to voicemail, so I called you. They tortured Jeff and sent his body back with their demands," Brian blurted, the panic clear in his voice.

This information froze me. If they were able to get Jeff, Dax's other right-hand man, then there was already a mole in our organization. The timing of Dax being taken and this going down couldn't be coincidental—it was too perfect. The biggest threat anyone faced getting to Tricks was that pink-haired, hell on wheels enforcer.

"Thank you for giving me this information. Where is Jeff's body now?" I asked, slipping into my computer chair.

"He was dumped out back of the tattoo shop, but when I got a call about it, I took him to the main warehouse by the pier. Should I call Brenda and let her know what happened?" Brian asked.

I rubbed my forehead as I thought this through. "No, give me until tomorrow before we say anything. We need to keep this as quiet as possible. There's no telling who the leak could be."

"You got it boss. Oh, is Dax with you? It's just odd I couldn't reach her."

"She's not with me at the moment, but I know where she is. When I pick her up, I'll make sure to fill her in on what's going on," I said, determination flooding my veins.

It was midnight by the time I pulled up to the warehouse that Brian dropped the body off at. Cutting the engine to my bike, I hung my helmet on the handlebar before getting off. The two guards stationed at the door nodded to me as one entered the code and opened the door to let me in. The building was quiet other than the clanking of my boots against the metal walkway to the cold storage area, and the only light was from the intermittent emergency floor lights.

When I reached the door at the end of the hall, I pulled out my key card and swiped it, then entered the passcode. The door slid open, and I descended down a flight of steps into an open room filled with crates full of contraband. Some were our own, others were product that we were moving for other clients. Reaching the large walk-in freezer, I pulled out my keys and unlocked the padlock, then unlatched the door. I placed the padlock back, blocking the latch from engaging again. Flicking on the light, I found a table with Jeff's body laying on it.

The poor bastard was hardly recognizable with how

much they'd worked him over. If I hadn't already known who I was looking at, I wasn't sure I would have been able to figure it out. He was naked, blood covering his body from where they'd carved AN EYE FOR AN EYE into his torso. His eyes had also been removed, just in case we didn't get the first message. Brian had already sent me a picture of the note that was jammed down his throat.

'*We seek retribution for Benny. Give us Dax or be ready to lose everything.*'

If the De León cartel thought Two Tricks would hand over one of his people to keep himself safe, they had another thing comin'—Tricks didn't bow to threats. The cartel didn't like how big the Hidden Empire had gotten, but they had no reason to outright challenge us, being on the East Coast. Seemed now their plan was to make shit up and start a war, whether we liked it or not.

Knowing Dax my whole life, I knew that she would never kill someone without just cause. She also wouldn't have gotten caught doing it. Dax might be wild, but if she let you in her huge heart, her love was astounding. I clenched my hands into fists as my anger at her being taken from me bowled over me.

I'd been in love with that woman my whole life, but she had made it clear that she would never settle down, that she thought love was foolish and made you do stupid things. All she wanted was loyalty, to trust you would never turn your back on her. She may not have seen that my loyalty came with my heart, but she had both, and now that she was ripped from my side, I couldn't seem to think straight.

This wasn't a problem I could manage on my own. I needed her by my side. Her wicked mind would be able to figure out how to fix this; my world was behind the scenes putting her plan into action. The Hidden Empire and Two

Tricks wouldn't be where they were today without Dax dealing with shit like this. Spinning on my heel, I marched out of the freezer and locked it up once again.

It was time to do something drastic and get my girl back where she belonged.

Chapter Eighteen
Dax

The sound of someone knocking on my door made me groan and roll over, pulling my pillow over my head. When nothing followed, I assumed the person who was disturbing my sleep had left, but I was not so lucky. Moments later, my door was opened—even though I was pretty sure I'd locked it—followed quickly by my covers being ripped off me.

"What the fuck?!" I cried, tossing my pillow in the direction that I thought the offender would be as I cracked my eyes open.

"*Loba*, that is not a nice way to greet someone," Cognac said, grinning at me.

I growled at him as he placed the pillow on the foot of my bed and walked over to open my blinds.

"What is with you people and being awake so early?" I muttered, rubbing my face with my hands.

Cognac reached out and ruffled my hair, grinning down at me. "How do you know it's early? There is no clock in this room."

Slapping his hand away, I glowered at him. "Trust me, my internal clock is never wrong. I bet it's sometime before ten o'clock." Cognac blinked at me, surprised, telling me that I was right. "Is there a reason that you're waking me up, or are you just a sadist who enjoys pissing me off?"

"I'm your babysitter today, and there are just so many fun things I want to do with you." He sat on my bed, a wide smile on his lips.

"Yeah... I'm not having sex with you," I said, crossing my arms.

"As much as I dream about the day that will happen, that wasn't quite what I had in mind. Thing is, I have to check the perimeter of the compound today and figured you might want to join me."

"Why would I want to do that?" I asked, feeling like he was holding something back.

"Oh, did I not mention that we would have to take an ATV out across our eight hundred acres of land? Hmm, I would have guessed by your car that you had a thing for speed and adrenaline," Cognac said with a shrug of his shoulder, getting off the bed. "But if you would rather be trapped in the garage with Sprocket for another day..."

Not that I didn't enjoy spending time with Sprocket, but the bait for getting out and having fun was just too strong. "Fine, I'll join you, just give me a chance to change."

"Ah yes," Cognac said, snapping his fingers. "Tilly dropped off a few bags of things for you downstairs. Just another incentive to get you out of bed."

I scrunched up my face in a frown at him, irritated that I was playing right into his hand... but I really wanted to wear normal clothes that fit.

Popping out of the bed, I raced out of the room and was

downstairs before he even stood up. I saw the shopping bags on the pool table and headed right for them. Digging through the bags, I grinned, seeing things that every badass chick needed for her wardrobe—distressed jeans, leather pants, sassy graphic tees that were bleached and cut up, and finally, a leather jacket.

"I think that's the first time I've seen you smile that doesn't involve food or coffee," Void said from the kitchen.

My head snapped up in his direction, yet again pissed that these guys could sneak up on me so easily. Void walked over to me and handed over a mug full of steaming coffee.

I looked at it, then him, with a raised eyebrow. "What's that for?"

"It's morning and you haven't had any yet," Void said with a shrug. "If you don't want it, that's fine—I'll just dump it out."

"Like hell you will!" I snapped, grabbing the mug from him. "How could you even think to toss out perfectly good coffee? What kind of heathen are you?"

"I'm not a heathen, little demon, I'm just not a crazed caffeine addict like you. Most normal people can survive without needing coffee injected into their veins," he grumbled. "By the way, don't think I've forgotten about winning our little bet—you'll be with us for the next thirty days. I already shared the news with the others at breakfast."

Taking a huge gulp of my coffee, I glared at him over the rim. "You don't seriously expect me to leave everything for the next month because I couldn't beat a trained MMA fighter, do you?"

Void gave me a grin that was mostly teeth. "Been snooping around, I see. Well, that should teach you to make a bet you know you can't win, unless Two Tricks' enforcer isn't a woman of her word."

Letting out a growl, I squared up to him. "If you know anything about me from all your research, you know I never go back on my word. What I really need to do is challenge you to a rematch and kick your ass."

Void just shook his head with a smirk on his lips. "Sorry, little demon, I don't need a rematch. I got what I wanted the first time around." He leaned down so we were nose to nose. "I don't start fights I can't win."

Booping me on the nose, he headed out of the house.

"AHHH!" I yelled as I snatched up the bags of clothes and headed for Eagle's room, not wanting to go all the way upstairs to mine where Cognac might be waiting for a striptease. If Void thought just because I wouldn't go against my word on this bet it didn't mean I wouldn't make him change his mind. I would make the next month hell until he sent me away himself.

Making sure the room was empty and I wasn't going to get snuck up on, I tossed off my clothes. Rooting through the bags, I found a handful of silky and lacy underwear that I couldn't help but roll my eyes at. I never understood why women invested in the stuff when normal underwear worked just as well. Pulling out a tank top that caught my eye, I smiled. It was all black, but on the back, the straps were made up of a collage of embroidered skulls in white. Slipping it on, I grabbed a pair of skinny jeans that had rips and alternative band patches sewn on them. I had to hand it to Tilly, she had great taste.

Dressed, I looked at the mess I made with my clothes, old and new, on the floor and all over Eagle's bed. All too pleased with myself, I left it, knowing he would be pissed when he found it.

Back in the living room, I saw Cognac packing stuff up

in a cooler, not noticing me right away. I watched as he put sandwiches, snacks, and various drinks in

"Did I miss the part where we are going on a picnic?" I asked.

"Well, you said I couldn't eat you, so I figured I would pack something else," Cognac answered without missing a beat.

I couldn't help the laughter that popped out of my mouth at his statement. Cognac was the epitome of a high school jock who thought he could get any girl he wanted with his smooth moves.

"Be honest—you're only interested in me because you can't have me. If I was easy, then you would be bored and move on to someone else," I challenged.

Cognac stopped and looked at me with raised eyebrows. "*Loba*, does that mean you're going to let me have my way with you so I'll leave you alone? Because I am all for that plan."

"Keep dreaming, buddy," I scoffed as I grabbed the boots Sprocket gave me yesterday.

"Trust me, you are the center of all my dreams, *loba*. I'm just waiting for you to realize that what we had on the dance floor wasn't fake. The connection we have can't be denied, no matter how hard you try," Cognac said, winking at me as he set the lid on the cooler.

"That's cute that you think that, really, but I don't do anything but casual hook-ups. I've only dated one guy, and that lasted two weeks before I caught him messing around with another girl. Things are just so much easier without the extra baggage when we both know all we want is to get off. Sex is a need. Why make it more complicated?"

Cognac just looked at me for a moment, the silence heavy between us. "I don't think I've ever heard such a jaded woman before. Come on, open the door for me, would ya? Let's get this day started."

Mildly surprised that he let the subject drop, I shrugged and held open the front door for him. The more I could lull him into believing that I wasn't a threat now that I'd supposedly agreed to stay for a month, the better. If they wanted to willingly take me out into the wilderness of their compound, that's on them. I told them upfront that I was gonna get out of this place, and this just seemed so perfect. If I could take out Cognac and steal the ATV, then I'd be well on my way to getting free.

It worried me how often I had to remind myself that I was a prisoner here and that these men were holding me captive. They wanted to use me against Two Tricks, and I couldn't let that happen. Not that I would ever give up any information, but it'd look bad if word got out that I had been kidnapped. My reputation was something I had worked to build and enforce for years; I couldn't afford to let myself become so easily distracted by this biker gang.

The ATV was parked in front of the house, and I was shocked to see it wasn't just your typical recreational vehicle. No, this was a tactical ATV like the military used in desert missions. It had two front seats and a short bed full of supplies that would be needed to repair the fence. It had a roll cage with a sun screen over the top to provide some shade while driving, but otherwise, it was open.

"Coming?" Cognac asked as he hopped into the driver's seat.

Jogging down the porch steps, I grabbed the roll cage and jumped in. I couldn't hold back the smile on my face at the excitement I was feeling at taking this baby out for a spin.

"Here, you're gonna want these," Cognac said, handing me a pair of aviator mirror-finish sunglasses.

"How do I look?" I asked, giving him my best duck-lips pose.

"Like the dangerously hot woman I know you are, *loba*," Cognac chuckled as he started up the diesel engine.

Looking over at the garage, I saw Sprocket leaning against one of the open doors. Feeling cheeky, I blew him a kiss and waved as Cognac peeled out, kicking up rocks from the driveway. Sprocket just shook his head and went back to work without even waving back.

Rude!

Leaning forward, Cognac turned on the radio and cranked the volume so it was blasting AC/DC. He immediately started drumming on the steering wheel and singing along. I was impressed—he had a good voice with a slight growl to it that fit the feel of the song perfectly. A fan of hard rock myself, I joined in, jamming out as we headed off into the wilderness of their compound.

Being so close to the foothills of the mountains, the ground was hilly with hard soil and full of scrub brush and pine trees. I couldn't really picture this being a cattle ranch with how barren and dried out everything was. Granted, it had been a very dry summer with hardly any rain, but still. I pictured more bright green pasture lands and open rolling hills when I thought *ranch*. Guess that's what I get for being a city girl and never really traveling much out of L.A.

Cognac cut across the ground, clearly very familiar with where we were going, until we reached the tall chain link fence. It seemed they'd taken a nod from the prison system in how they designed their defenses. The fence was twelve feet tall, at least, with barbed wire over the top and motion detectors at regular intervals. This was not what I'd pictured when Cognac said we needed to check the fence, but I shouldn't have been surprised—being the largest MC came with having enemies who wanted to take your spot in the world.

Apparently, my escape wasn't going to be quite as easy as I hoped.

Chapter Nineteen
Cognac

As much as she tried to hide it, Dax was angry when she saw the fence that we had put up along the inner part of our eight hundred acres. I wasn't even going to mention that this was only the four hundred acre mark and that we had even more traps set up outside the safe zone. This was the area that we kept protected for our use as a community.

We all knew that she wasn't going to willingly stay with us for a month, no matter what bet she made. If we had any chance of making our plan work, we needed to get her to feel like she wasn't a prisoner so that running away fell from the top of her list. Hearing her talk about how she viewed relationships was a slap in the face, though. Most of my life I'd viewed things the same way, but sitting here next to this tiny woman that was turning our world upside down made me think differently for the first time in years.

Dax was different than any woman we had ever spent time with. She was smart, cunning, and lethal. The fact that she took on Void and only ended up with a bruised cheek was a miracle. And I knew he didn't hold back, because he didn't understand the concept of not giving his all in a fight. I could see the respect in his gaze when he looked at her now, and that wasn't something he ever gave out to women. If there was anyone more closed off than Dax to relationships, it was Void.

Picasso was still keeping his distance for the most part, not completely convinced that this was the right choice, but he wouldn't deny his brother anything. Eagle was over the moon about this girl, the likes of which I'd never seen before. At dinner last night he would have killed Void for leaving a mark on her if she hadn't told him off. Eagle was a scary bastard, but she went toe to toe with him, and it was a sight to see. Our beautiful *loba* was indeed a wolf in a woman's body, and I couldn't wait until I got her to unleash that passion on me.

"So, what exactly are we looking for as we 'check' the fence?" Dax asked using air quotes.

I turned down the music since it seemed she was interested in talking. "We need to make sure there's no damaged areas and that all the motion sensors are working. Rooster said that there was a sensor down, so I figured checking out the rest made sense."

"Ah, so you have a security room then," Dax ventured, glancing at me out of the corner of her eye.

"Crafty little minx. You're going to need to try harder than that to get that kind of information out of me, *loba*." I grinned.

Dax shifted in her seat to look at me easier. "What does that mean, anyway?"

"*Loba?*" I asked, knowing full well what she meant.

Rolling her eyes, she huffed at me. "Yes, *loba*. You've

been calling me that since I got here, figured I should know what it means."

"What do you think it means?" I asked, enjoying pushing her buttons.

I could see her frowning at me out of the corner of my eye, but I kept my eyes on the fence as we continued along, attempting to do the job we came out here for.

"If I find out that it means something nasty or rude towards women, I will cut off your dick that you love so much," Dax growled.

My lips twitched in a grin as I fought to keep my face blank.

"Hmm... *low-bah*," Dax said, drawing the word out. "I'm gonna guess it's some kind of endearment, like *babe* or something as equally awful."

"Nope."

In a flash, she reached over and grabbed my nipple, giving it a good twist.

"FUCK!" I cried, jerking the wheel and almost crashing us into a tree.

Thankfully we weren't going that fast, and I swerved out of the way in time, then slammed on the brakes.

"What the hell was THAT!" I demanded, glaring down at her.

"If you weren't being such an ass and just told me already, we wouldn't be in this situation," Dax retorted with her arms crossed and a cocked brow.

"*Mujer loca*," I muttered, rubbing my chest. "*Loba* means wolf, and in this moment I wish I'd gone with something more vindictive."

Dax flashed me a blinding smile and settled back into her seat. "Now, was that so hard?"

I humphed and starting us rolling again, but inside I

couldn't be more pleased with how tenacious she was. If there was ever a chance for a woman to handle all of us, it would be this woman right here.

"I approve of your choice in nickname," Dax announced. "I'm glad you didn't pick anything cute and sappy."

Laughing, I shook my head. "Even if you didn't like the name *loba*, I wasn't going to stop using it. You don't get a choice in what I call you, no matter how much you abuse me over it. I have a feeling that the others will feel the same about their chosen nicknames."

"We'll see about that. Picasso tried to call me 'sweetpea.' There is no way in hell I'm going to let that stand."

"Picasso, for all of his artistic talent, does not have a way with words, so I'm not surprised," I said absently as I spotted an anomaly in the fence up ahead.

Gunning the ATV, I pulled us up to the spot and got out, seeing the chain link gaping open where it'd been cut. I looked up and noted that the motion sensors to the left and right were still active, and there was no sign that they had been tampered with. Going back to the ATV, I pulled out the remote laptop that paired with the security system and got diagnostics of the past twenty-four hours. I glanced up, seeing Dax looking at the fence and surrounding area outside, looking at something on the ground.

"Did you find something?" I questioned as the computer booted up.

She squatted down as if to get a closer look, so I gave up waiting for her to tell me and walked over to check it out myself. Peering over her shoulder, I saw footprints in the dirt, but it looked like it was only one person. Spinning around, I looked on the inside of the fence and saw the tracks heading back towards the compound. Cursing, I ran over to the ATV and grabbed the radio to alert the others that someone had broken in, but I never got the chance as I was struck from behind.

Goddamnit! I should've known better than to turn my back on a *loba* who was waiting for the perfect time to strike.

Chapter Twenty
Dax

"Weston!" I gasped as Cognac crumbled to the ground.

I couldn't believe my eyes. Even though I'd only been gone for less than four days, so much had happened. Wes turned to me and scooped me up in his arms, clutching me tightly to his chest as he buried his face into my neck. Stunned, never having seen him act like this before, I didn't fight his hold.

"I can't believe I let them take you, shortcake," Wes murmured into my neck.

Unsure of what else to do, I hugged him back just as tightly. "They didn't hurt me. I'm okay, Westy."

Setting me back down, he pulled zip ties out of his back pocket and secured Cognac's hands and feet. Then he picked me up and set me on the bed of the ATV, kneeling down and pulling off my boot. His fingers brushed against my skin just above where the ankle monitor was, as if he was afraid to set it off.

"They've never used it," I told him, giving him a small smile when he looked up at me. "Did you find a way to get it off of me?"

"Yes and no," Wes sighed. "I can mask it long enough for us to get it off, but we need a magnetic key. Each key is custom to each ankle monitor so the person who is wearing it can't just get ahold of any random key and use it. With the app, I can make you disappear long enough for us to figure something out. The trick was getting you and one of the leaders with the app out of here before anyone noticed, but it seems you did that for me."

A lightbulb went off in my head. "You disabled the motion sensor!"

Wes nodded as he stood and went through Cognac's pockets until he found his cell phone. Then he tested each of Cognac's fingers until the right one unlocked the phone. Swiftly, he went through the apps until he found the one he needed as he pulled out a cord from the tactical vest he was wearing. Weston was never the one to be on the front lines —that was always my job—but we'd both trained to be ready for any situation, a requirement for Two Tricks. Grabbing the laptop, I watched as his fingers flew over the keyboard, bypassing the security and gaining access to their whole compound's system.

"I'm going to cause a major diversion in the compound that should keep them busy long enough for us to get to a safehouse. I don't want to risk taking you back home or to the shop because that will be the first place they'll look," Wes said, not looking up from his work.

I nodded. "We can't go to any of Tricks' warehouses either in case masking my signal doesn't work. Guess you weren't so crazy for making us have safehouses all over the state."

A loud siren blared behind us, making me jump.

"Don't worry, it's just me," Wes reassured as he plugged in the phone, hacking into that next. "Just a few more seconds and we should be good. Got it! Okay, you jump in the driver's seat, and I'll get him strapped in back here so we don't lose him with your crazy-ass driving."

"You're always so mean to me, Wes." I pouted, even though I could only hold it for a second before a smile bloomed on my lips.

Hopping down, I slipped my foot back in my boot and tied it back up before vaulting into the driver's seat. I of course had to move the seat all the way up and lower the steering wheel, but none of that mattered as I turned the key and the engine rumbled to life. The back bed had three-foot sides, so I wasn't too worried about him falling out once Wes got him strapped in.

"Oh, make sure to keep the cooler—it's full of food and drinks," I called over my shoulder.

Moments later, Wes was by the fence with a set of bolt cutters, making a big enough opening for me to drive though. It took longer than I wanted it to, knowing that we had limited time to get the fuck out of here before they noticed we were gone.

"Cognac! Cognac, come in! Everything back here is going crazy, Eagle thinks we're under attack by Two Tricks. We need you and Dax back here now!"

I looked down at the radio for a moment, unsure of what to do. The voice was so frenzied, I couldn't tell if I knew who it was. Reaching down and grabbing the radio from the floor, I rolled my shoulders and readied myself for the performance of my life.

"Help! They are shooting at us! Please, we need backup. Cognac ran out of bullets. We're on the east side along the fence line. Please, there's too many of them!" I shouted into the walkie-talkie, revving the engine so it sounded like we were running for our lives.

There was a pause, then Eagle's voice came across the radio. "Dax, who is after you? What can you tell us?"

"It's the Mad Dogs!" I answered, knowing that the two MCs didn't like each other.

The Phantom Saints had pushed them out of the L.A. area when they grew in power, and Mastiff, their president, didn't take it well. There had been rumblings recently that they were going to make a move to reclaim their territory.

"There has to be twenty of them or so after us! Cognac took out a few, but they are gaining on us. Please help!"

I pushed the desperation in my voice, knowing that in reality I never would have let anyone think I was that weak. But I really needed them to believe what I was saying and keep them busy while we got away.

"Hang in there, little hellcat, we're coming," Eagle said, a darkness in his voice that I could pick up even over the radio.

Tossing the walkie-talkie out of the ATV, I flipped it into drive, slamming my foot on the gas and shooting through the opening Wes made us. Pausing long enough for him to jump in, I fishtailed as the tires kicked up dirt into a cloud. Laughing, I grinned as we flew across the open land to freedom, cranking up the music once again.

"Fuck, Dax!" Wes yelled. He held onto the roll cage for dear life as I sent us airborne over the crest of a hill, crashing back to the ground with a whoop. "Do you have to make everything into a life-or-death situation?"

"How else do we know if we've lived life to the fullest? When my time comes, I want to have no doubt that I took advantage of all life had to offer. Besides, when else am I gonna run away from a biker gang and return the favor by kidnapping one of their guys?" I asked, horns blaring as I cut across a four-lane road.

"Not all of us see the fun in living our lives like that," Wes grumbled, checking behind us at Cognac.

Rolling my eyes, I gave him a pointed look. "Says the guy who just snuck into a biker gang's compound with no backup to get me out. How exactly was that plan gonna work if we hadn't happened to fall into your lap?"

"If you must know, I was taking a play out of your book and was just gonna wing it when I got to that point." Wes shrugged.

My lips pulled into a wide grin at his words as we crossed through a river, soaking us as water sprayed everywhere.

"Was that really necessary? There was a bridge," Wes griped, wiping off his face.

"Please refer back to my earlier statement," I chirped with a wink.

Wes just shook his head and pointed to the left. "Take this road until it ends at a cabin. That's our destination."

Pulling onto the uneven dirt road, I slowed, not wanting to draw any attention if there were surrounding cabins or campsites. I shouldn't have been too worried, though, seeing as we'd gone up into the mountain range with towering pine trees, the air cooling with the shade.

We hit a big rut in the road and a loud grunt came from the back, letting us know that Cognac was awake. I peeked over my shoulder to find him glaring up at me, teeth bared around the gag that Wes had put on him. And just because of who I am, I gave him a wink. He thrashed around in the back, but he didn't get very far with how securely Weston had tied him to the bed.

After a few more miles down a road that would have killed anything besides a truck—or an ATV—a small log cabin appeared. It was nestled in the pine trees, the picture of secluded bliss with its simplistic appearance. There was a covered port that I parked the ATV under, silence descending upon us after I killed the engine. I hopped out, stretching as I took in the small patio that had two wooden chairs on it, setting the tone of the cabin.

Heading up the stairs, I examined the doorframe for our typical spot to hide the keys. Spying the small etched double-spade, I pushed on it, and the wooden compartment popped open, showing a lockbox with the keys. I put in the code and snatched the keys, unlocking the door.

"Don't be a dick and I won't knock you out again," Wes growled at Cognac as he hauled him out of the bed of the ATV.

Wes cut the ties around Cognac's legs and pulled him to his feet, shoving him forward. Trusting Wes to manage Cognac, I entered, taking in the open concept of the safehouse. My eye was drawn to the stone fireplace with the simple brown couch in front of it. The kitchen was to the right, simple and clean, with an old-fashioned woodburning stove. I remembered when Wes talked us into making this into a safehouse because it was run all on solar power and natural resources. Totally off the grid. The bedroom was up the stairs in a loft area that was open to the rest of the cabin.

Weston shoved Cognac into one of the kitchen chairs and tied him to it. This was not the best place for holding a captive, but it was definitely going to be hard to find if things went according to plan.

Then I would have to decide what to do with Cognac. The simplest choice was to just kill him. Although there might be a way to use him so they didn't retaliate if we let him go and both went our separate ways. Ambling over, I pulled the gag out of his mouth and perched on the kitchen table so we were eye to eye.

"*Loba*," Cognac said, his eyes searching mine.

"Allow me to introduce you to Weston Price, my business partner, best friend, and left hand to Two Tricks," I said. Wes hissed at me, upset I was sharing information. "Wes, this is Cognac, treasurer to the Phantom Saints and all-around ladies' man who believes he will one day talk me into sleeping with him."

Cognac and Wes looked at each other for a few moments, their gazes unreadable. Cognac broke the tension first, putting on his flirty grin and glancing over at me.

"It seems we underestimated your warning. How the hell did you two even coordinate a plan like this without us knowing?" Cognac asked.

Hmm, they thought we'd planned this somehow. No sense in telling him it was a total fluke of right place, right time.

"As Picasso once said, you don't get to have my job without having a few tricks of your own." I smiled, resting my chin on my hand. "Now, it seems that we need a special key to get this damn thing off me. You wouldn't happen to have it, would you?"

"Do you really think I would make it that simple for you to run away from us? Before you ask, no. I'm not going to tell you who has it, either." Cognac grinned, far too pleased with himself for a guy who was tied to a chair.

Weston leaned against the table just behind me and nudged me with his shoulder. "It seems as though he's forgotten that you're Two Tricks' enforcer."

Never once had I questioned my place or the job that I

did, but somehow the thought of using my normal tactics on Cognac didn't sit right with me. Maybe it could be that they hadn't used force on me while I was their guest, but I wasn't sure I could threaten it out of him.

Leaning back, I let my head fall to Weston's shoulder and looked up at him. "I don't want to spoil all my fun in one go. Let's let him sit for a while as the reality that the roles are now reversed sinks in. Besides, I'm sure you have a lot to fill me in on after being gone for so long."

Cognac narrowed his eyes as Wes wrapped his arms around my waist, holding me to his chest as he rested his head in the crook of my neck. Typically I wasn't one to be all touchy-feely, but I'd truly missed Weston, and it had been a very long time since I hadn't seen or at least talked to him every day. Having him yanked out of my life bothered me far more than I thought it would.

"I have something slightly different in mind to talk to you about," Wes said, his voice muffled by my skin, his lips sending shivers down my spine.

Frowning, I tried to pull him away so I could get a better look at him, but when he lifted his head, it was to plant his lips on mine. Stunned, I didn't move. My mind was racing, trying to catch up to what was happening. He pulled back only enough to shift me so that I was facing him as he cupped my face, looking into my eyes, searching.

"I didn't think it was possible, but I think I just shocked you into silence." Wes grinned.

Growling, I grabbed the front of his vest, pulling him back to me before I could overthink this. "This better not be a fucking joke, Westy, or I will cut off your balls so the world will never be inflicted with your offspring."

Stroking my cheek with one of his thumbs, he rested his

forehead against mine. "No joke. Just way overdue in making it happen, shortcake."

I grabbed the back of his neck and slammed my lips on his, devouring his mouth as if I only had moments to live. He slid one hand into my hair and grabbed a handful, pulling my head back so he could kiss down my neck. The other free hand slipped up the back of my shirt, his large palm pulling me flush against him so he could rub his jean-clad cock against my core.

"Fuck!" I cried as I fumbled to get the tactical vest off him, pulling at the zipper.

Sensing my frustration, he pulled back and quickly managed the vest, tossing it along with his shirt behind him before pulling mine off.

"You have got to be kidding me right now!" Cognac groaned. "I thought you said you didn't want to torture me right now. This is just cruel—even for you, *loba*."

I flicked my gaze over to him, but when Wes bit down on my nipple, all thoughts of our onlooker flew out of my mind. Combing my fingers into Weston's perfectly placed hair, I held on tight as he bit and pinched my nipples at the same time, making me buck under him.

"Holy shit, Wes!"

"I have waited long enough to have you, so I'm going to need all your attention on me, shortcake," Wes purred as he kissed a trail down my stomach, pushing me back on the table.

Flicking the button on my jeans open, he made short work of yanking them and my underwear off me. I lay there, bare to him, grinning as he took a moment just to gaze at me. With both his hands, he traced over my body as if he were memorizing it. When he brushed his thumbs along my inner thigh, I squirmed, but I wasn't going to give in and beg like I could see in his eyes he wanted me to. This girl didn't beg for anything, and I knew I could hold out longer than he could if push came to shove.

Thankfully, I didn't have to worry as he dropped to his knees and pulled my legs open. Pulling me to the edge of the table, he tossed my legs over each of his shoulders, supporting my weight. I craned my neck, holding his gaze as he lapped at my clit, sending me slamming back onto the table.

"God yes, just keep doing whatever that is," I gasped as his tongue swirled around my nub, sending a shockwave of sensation through me.

Trying to keep myself from leaping off the table as his teeth grazed my clit, I grabbed the sides of the table, digging my nails into the wood as an orgasm slammed into my body. Unrelenting, Wes dragged out the high as long as he could, slipping in two fingers and bringing another level of ecstasy. Finished, he cupped my ass, lifting me from the table until I wrapped my arms around his neck. Fire blazed in his eyes as he kissed me, still covered in my essence, which made it far more intimate.

Slowly, he lowered me, and I felt the blunt head of his dick fill me until I was seated against his pelvic bone. Locking my ankles behind him, I leaned back a little to get a better angle and rocked my hips, causing friction but not letting him pull out of me. I needed to feel every inch of him right now, claiming this cock that no other woman would have again as my own.

"Dax, you're killin' me, you're squeezing me so tight," Wes growled.

I gave him a toothy grin. "I just need to make sure your dick remembers where it belongs in case it has any questions."

Weston met my gaze, and the level of seriousness made me still my movement. "Dax Rose Blackmore, I have always been yours. There has never been anyone else."

The rush of emotions I was feeling at his words hit me like a semi. I believed every word he said, and as much as it filled my heart with warmth, it also freaked me the fuck out. After Devin, I didn't do love—it hurt too much when they left you. Weston had been my rock, the constant in my life, and I loved him, but it wasn't the way he was talking about right now.

Was I even able to love like that?

Seeing that I was on the verge of a freak-out, he spun and slammed me against the kitchen wall, shocking me out of my thoughts. He once again buried his head in my neck, but this time he latched on with his teeth as he thrust into me, causing me to grunt in pleasure. My fingers raked down his back, and I knew he would bear my marks when this was all over. Then I caught sight of Cognac watching, his eyes glazed over in lust, his arms straining at his restraints.

Seemed this was an effective type of torture when used on the right people.

Wes sped up, causing me to break my connection with Cognac and give myself over to the pleasure of this beautiful man thrusting away in me. Together we came, shouting, panting, and wringing out every ounce of pleasure we could from each other. Without even looking, I knew there was going to be a perfect bruise of Weston's teeth on my neck, but I was oddly pleased about it.

As Wes set me down, I leaned against the wall to make sure I had my legs firmly under me before moving. Once I was sure my body remembered how to function, I pulled Wes down for a gentle kiss before glancing around him.

Catching Cognac's eye, I sauntered over to him and sat on his lap, throwing my arms around his neck.

"Now, did you want to tell me who has the key? Or is there another way to get this off me? If you tell me, I promise I'll take care of that stiff problem you have going on. I can only imagine how uncomfortable that must be for you," I said, pouting my lips at him.

Cognac growled at me, narrowing his eyes. "*Loba*, when you meet my cock for the first time, it won't be with me strapped to a chair after seeing you fuck your best friend. I might be a manwhore, but even I have standards."

"Suit yourself," I said with a shrug, standing and then looking at Wes. "I'm gonna go take a quick shower. You wanna join me and conserve water?"

"Of course. We have to do our bit for the environment," he said, smirking at Cognac as he followed after me.

Chapter Twenty-one
Dax

Freshly showered and with a hot cup of coffee in my hands, I curled up on one of the chairs on the porch. Weston sagged in his chair opposite me, rubbing his chin as if he was unsure about something.

"What's wrong?" I finally asked since he refused to talk first.

Wes sighed and raked his hands through his hair. "Jeff is dead. He was tortured and dropped off at the shop with a note jammed down this throat. Seems the De León cartel believes you killed Diego's son Benny while he was in L.A. for vacation a few months back."

Stunned, I paused with my cup hovering almost to my lips. Rage boiled through my veins when I registered the words that Wes just told me. Seconds later, I was on my feet and the coffee mug was smashed against the side of the cabin.

"WHAT THE FUCK DO YOU MEAN JEFF IS DEAD!" I screamed, balling my hands into fists so tight I could feel my nails biting into my skin. "How the hell could I kill their son when I have no idea who he is or what the bastard even looks like? You better know what's going on, Weston."

Wes stood and walked over to me, putting his hands on my shoulders so he could look me right in the eye. "They are finally making their move, Dax. If they have any chance of getting to Two Tricks, they know they have to get you out of the way first. We've found every person that they've tried to go behind our backs and work with. Diego De León isn't one of the biggest drug bosses on the East Coast for no reason. With the US border crackdown, they need smugglers, and that is the number one thing the Hidden Empire controls."

I yanked myself out of Weston's hold, not wanting him to calm me down, and paced the porch. "So what if I supposedly killed their son? He was in L.A., on our turf, and didn't say anything to us. None of our people or connections would give a shit that I supposedly killed someone from a rival cartel. On the other hand, the De Leóns have no grounds to kill off one of my right-hand men —in MY CITY!"

"That's just it, though. They came in while you were gone and killed one of your inner circle. If they can get to the enforcer's men, then they can get to anyone. Someone is also spreading rumors about the fact that you're missing. I've done my best to put a stop to it, but my words won't hold them over for long. They need to see you," Wes stated, leaning back against the rail, arms crossed and a frown marring his handsome face.

I turned and punched the cabin wall until both of my hands ached at the unforgiving surface. Wes knew better than to stop me when I got like this, even though I could feel his disapproving gaze on my back.

"That's the catch twenty-two of it all, isn't it. If I can't get this motherfucking tracker off, there's no way I can deal with things back home."

"If I might interject here for a moment, I might have a solution," Cognac said.

Snapping my head around, I found him leaning against the doorjamb, hands in his jean pockets and a grin on his face.

"How the fuck did you get out of your bindings?" I gaped.

Cognac walked over to me and bent down until he was right next to the side of my face, whispering into my ear. "*Loba*, you would be surprised at the things I could teach you if you let me."

Then he licked the shell of my ear, causing me to shudder as a thrill went through my body. Yes, even though I had just been thoroughly fucked, his body called to mine—it had ever since that dance the first night we met. He pulled back, lust glowing in his eyes as he winked at me before standing to his full height.

Weston was not so easily pacified with that answer and slammed Cognac against the wall with his arm pinned behind him. "Why the hell should we listen to you? For all we know, you could be working with them! It seems just too coincidental that she gets kidnapped the same time they start this shit."

"Now I understand why you're so hard to impress, *loba*. After seeing the connection between you two and the lovely porno you put on for me, we've got our work cut out for us to get you to stay," Cognac said, ignoring everything Weston just said.

"As for what I was saying before Westy here rudely interrupted me, all you have to do is have Two Tricks agree to talk with Eagle, and we'll be more than happy to take your anklet off."

"I have to agree with Wes on this—the timing of everything is just too convenient. Gabriella comes to see me with the one person who I hate for stealing my twin from me, then my best friend invites me to a party at her house. Harper has no clue about Two Tricks or the Hidden Empire, other than they exist. Tie in the fact that Gabriella set it up so you guys could meet me—I'm sorry, kidnap me... There's not much here to go on that makes me think bringing you to Two Tricks—the best kept secret—is a great idea," I mused as I resumed my pacing.

Cognac gave me a heavy sigh, and quick as lightning, he had Weston on the floor. "Sorry man, but my shoulder was starting to fall asleep and I hate it when it gets all tingly." He flopped into the chair Wes had been sitting in and scratched the scruff on his chin. "I see your point, Dax, but the whole time you've been with us we have done everything in our power to make you comfortable. Other than keeping an eye on you and the ankle monitor, we haven't treated you like a prisoner. That has to count for something."

"What is it exactly that Eagle wants from Tricks anyway?" I asked, curious.

"I'll let him tell you that. He and the others should be here soon," Cognac said with a yawn.

"S'cuse me, *what?!*" I demanded, marching up to him and grabbing the front of his t-shirt.

Reaching out, he scooped me up and pulled me into his lap, locking me in place with his arms. "When you passed out of our property, the tracker on the ATV was activated. I know your brooding stud over here checked it, but it wouldn't be detectable until it was triggered. Guess you should've ditched the ride if you didn't want to be followed."

I squirmed and kicked in Cognac's arms, growling. "You promised you wouldn't touch me unless I told you you could."

"True, but I changed my mind. After seeing you with Wessy boy, I'm a little worried you might never let me. So I'm just going to do it anyways or risk my opportunity being lost, *loba*," Cognac said, nuzzling into the back of my neck.

I tried to headbutt him, but he just shifted and tucked me in under his chin, humming with contentment.

"Are you just gonna let him do this to me, Wes?" I snarled, still not giving in. "If you don't help me get out of his arms, I'm going to dump everything out of your drawers and toss it around the room at home. Then I'll rearrange everything on your computer home screen. Don't test me, Weston!"

"She makes a mess in your room too, huh?" Eagle asked, coming out of the trees, gun at the ready with the rest of the guys flanking him.

Weston dropped to a knee behind the second chair and pulled out his own gun. I froze in Cognac's hold, unsure of what was going to happen next.

"Seems our little demon is causing all sorts of trouble today. I knew things had been going too smoothly," Void drawled as they fanned out to cover the whole porch.

"Can't say we weren't warned. Pretty sure the first thing out of her mouth was that she would raise hell." Eagle ginned as he lowered his gun. "I know it's just the two of you here, and clearly we outnumber you, especially since I have men waiting for my signal if need be. I figured we could talk about this like adults instead of needing to kill each other. See, the thing is, friend, we've all grown kinda fond of our little hellcat." Eagle shrugged, speaking to Wes.

"Perfect timing, pres," Cognac said, lifting me out of his lap and setting me on my feet. "*Loba* was just asking why it is that you need to meet with Two Tricks."

Weston looked at me, then the rest of the guys, and holstered his weapon. No matter how you looked at it, there wouldn't have been a chance in hell to get out of this alive if it came down to a shootout.

"Why don't I grab the cooler and we can all have lunch?" Cognac said, heading for the ATV.

What the actual fuck was going on right now? Was this another part of their plan? No, there's no way they could've known that Weston was coming for me. Wes was loyal to me through and through. But then how the hell did we end up in this situation?

"Dax, aren't you going to introduce us to your friend?" Sprocket asked when he reached me.

"No," I snapped, turning my back to him. "You can figure it out yourself."

"Really, I thought we'd gotten past all this attitude," Sprocket teased, putting his arm around me as he escorted me into the cabin like it was theirs.

Weston let out a bark of laughter. "Fat chance of that. She's been only getting sassier with age, trust me."

Once in the cabin, someone grabbed my hand and yanked me away from Sprocket, spinning me until I was up against the back of the couch. Eagle loomed over me, his eyes filled with anger as his hand surrounded my throat. He didn't put any pressure into the grip—just the knowledge he could was enough to keep my attention.

"Get. Your. Hands. Off. Her," Wes commanded, followed by the sound of a gun being cocked.

Eagle glanced at him for a moment but then brought his gaze right back to me. "I warned you that you could only push me so far, little hellcat. Not only did you run away and kidnap one of my men, but you left a fucking mess in my room for me to clean up. There will be consequences for your actions, no matter what this asshole thinks."

With those words, I noticed the other four guys had their guns trained on Weston, who had his gun up against Eagle's head.

"Oh, Eagle, you might want to address the fact that they fucked like rabbits not that long ago," Cognac piped up.

Eagle shifted so he could see him better. "What do you mean?"

"Little ol' Wessy here banged her good and hard right in front of me and again in the shower, making her scream loud enough I got jealous I couldn't watch." Cognac smirked as he saw me glaring daggers at him.

Wes made a move towards Cognac, but Void was right there blocking him, his gun inches away from his head. "If he moves, he won't make it out of this alive. Now tell him to stand down," Void commanded.

I licked my lips, as my mouth had gone dry at the horror of knowing Void would kill Weston without blinking an eye. But I couldn't lose Wes. There would be no way that I could survive living life without him in it, even more so after what had just happened between us.

"Put down the gun, Wes. Eagle still needs me, so he won't hurt me," I said, giving Wes a reassuring nod. "Besides, he knows if he did, I would kick his ass."

Weston locked eyes with me as if he was trying to read my soul, but he blinked and took a step back, slowly lowering his weapon. As the room seemed to breathe again, I grabbed Eagle's thumb and yanked it back, freeing my neck. Pulling the arm down, I kneed him in the stomach, causing him to grunt at the pain as he fell to his knees. Finishing it off, I punched him in the jaw, whipping his head back with a groan.

"Don't you ever threaten Weston's life again or I will end you without a second thought. He's off-limits if you ever want the hope of meeting Tricks!" I screamed right in his face, anger pouring out of me.

Seconds later, pain flooded my body, and I dropped to the ground as I started convulsing. Rolling my eyes up, I saw Picasso watching me with fury in his gaze and his phone in his hands.

The bastard used the shock collar on me.

Chapter Twenty-Two
Dax

As my body was shifted and picked up, I let out a loud groan of protest. Every muscle in my body was pissed that I'd been fucking electrocuted, and now I was practically helpless.

Void's icy blue eyes looked down at me with something I might count as concern. He carried me over to the couch, but instead of setting me on it, he held me in his lap like a baby, shifting me so my head rested against his shoulder as he wrapped his arms around my hips. It took me a moment to figure out that the pounding in my head was getting worse because of the shouting happening.

"What the fuck were you thinking?!" Eagle bellowed.

"There is no way in hell I was willing to let her get away with that! No one disrespects you like that, Eagle, I don't care who they are," Picasso shot back.

"So that whole thing about not torturing her because that's not what we do was bullshit? Because to me that looked like you just took her ass out to be a dick," Sprocket chimed in.

"Ah! Fuck you all, being blinded by some piece of ass," Picasso yelled, followed by the sound of something smashing. "I was against this plan from the beginning. We never should have brought her back with us. Now we have two of Two Tricks' people to hold hostage—he's got to do something about that, right?!"

"That just shows you know fuck all about Two Tricks," Wes bit out. "You think after this many years he's going to cave just because you have his enforcer and her business partner?"

"Nice try, asshole, but we both know that you are more than just her business partner. She wouldn't go to bat like that for just anyone. Besides, there's no way that you could have pulled that shit if you weren't in Two Tricks' inner circle yourself," Picasso challenged.

"Regardless, my point still stands. Tricks isn't going to give in because of this."

"Fine then. Seems with this new development, we just need to kill them both and send back their bodies to get our message across," Picasso snapped.

The sound of someone getting punched and crashing into something made me try to see what was going on. As I lifted my head from Void's shoulder, I saw Sprocket standing over Picasso, who had been laid out. To say that I was shocked that they were fighting amongst themselves over me was an understatement. It threw me for a loop.

"Picasso, go take a walk, and when you can be more reasonable, feel free to come back and apologize to Dax for your shit attitude," Sprocket growled.

Picasso picked himself up off the ground and looked at Eagle like he was waiting for him to tell Sprocket to back down, but Eagle just crossed his arms. I watched as Picasso stormed out of the cabin, slamming the door behind him. Eagle walked over to me and squatted down so we were eye level and reached out, grasping my ankle gently.

"I'm sorry he did that, hellcat. Don't get me wrong, you needed a good punishment for lashing out at me like that, but this was overkill," Eagle said, pinning me with a stern look.

I huffed, squirming in Void's hold even though my body screamed at me to stop moving. Void just grunted and maneuvered me so I was sitting up with my back flush with his chest but still locked in his hold.

"If I didn't have this fucking thing on me, none of this would have been an issue. Just so we're clear, this isn't all on me—if you hadn't all pulled your guns on Wes, I wouldn't have reacted so badly," I muttered, trying to pry Void's hands loose.

A hand cupped my chin and forced me to look Eagle in the eyes. "Don't run away from us with some other guy and I won't be so unreasonable."

"Okay, do you hear yourself right now? How is this my fault? I'm the one who was kidnapped and held against my will in your compound. Wes came to get me free, and we just happened to need Cognac to come with for insurance. I could've killed him and left him for you to find as you tried to come after me. Really, you should be thanking me right now," I said, slapping his hand away and glaring at him.

Eagle looked over at Cognac, who was sitting on the arm of the couch, twirling his gun like it was a toy.

"Nah, I don't think you could've killed him, little hellcat. I mean, look at that face—he's much too pretty to kill." Eagle grinned, and Cognac turned to wink at me.

Heaving a heavy sigh, I leaned back into Void, giving

into the fact I wasn't going anywhere. "Let's move on since we are getting nowhere with that topic. I'm finally ready to listen to your proposal."

Eagle stood and settled next to Void while Sprocket and Wes pulled over chairs from the kitchen.

"Can we expect loverboy to behave himself?" Void asked as he dipped his chin to rest it on my shoulder.

Wes slammed his chair down hard on the floor, drawing our attention. "I am perfectly capable of answering for myself, Cujo."

Not helping his case, Void growled at Wes, moving to pass me over to Eagle. "What did you just call me, etch-a-sketch?"

"Hey!" I yelled elbowing Void in the gut. "I did almost all of his tattoos, insulting them is insulting me!"

Void paused and looked down at me, then back at Wes, before settling back on the couch with a pout on his lips, pulling me back to him.

"Look at that—our little rebel has learned to tame the beast," Sprocket said, winking at me with a grin on his lips.

I stuck my tongue out at him, but he just shook his head. "I wouldn't do that—you never know what could happen to it, little rebel."

Eagle clapped his hands together loudly. "Could we try to keep on topic for just a moment?"

When we all fell silent, I wiggled so I could face him better, which also put me in a position that Void's dick was tucked against my ass cheeks. This caused him to nuzzle against my neck and then bite the shell of my ear. Batting him away, I raised an eyebrow at Eagle, hoping he would start talking.

"Everyone knows that the real person who is in control of the West Coast is Two Tricks and the Hidden Empire. I know everyone thinks that MCs should just stick to women, drugs, and guns, but why can't we be more? The Phantom Saints could really mean something in this town, except that Tricks has us blocked on all sides, forcing us to live up to that reputation," Eagle started, his eye watching me carefully for any chance I might give something away.

"As his enforcer, you offer protection to all the people that work with Two Tricks. Some of them even get some of your men to be on site at all times. I know you probably just see it as protecting your boss's investments, but it also makes the whole neighborhood safer. We had a hell of a time finding anything out because you have built up that kind of loyalty—not Tricks, Dax. You. Our original idea was to be able to join forces and combine what we do, mix our skills with Tricks' and make the empire bigger. To do that would take trusted men and women to control that much territory. I have a few gangs that I plan to take over and patch in as Phantoms, but I can't without pushback from your people."

"You're still not telling me what it is that you want, Eagle," I pushed. I knew exactly what he wanted from that little speech, but I needed him to say it out loud so there were no misconceptions. "Also, what do you mean by your 'original idea'? I'm guessing something changed."

Eagle rubbed the scruff on his chin, watching me with an expression I couldn't read. "Yes, things have changed because there was one thing that there was no way we could account for."

"Really, what could that be?" I mused, cocking my head to the side.

"They didn't count on a pint-sized hellion with a foul mouth and aggressive personality to end up turning them all into whipped puppies," Picasso said from behind us.

Eagle just grunted as Picasso grabbed a chair and sat on it backwards next to his brother.

"Think you can manage not to shock or shoot anyone while we talk?" Eagle asked. Picasso's answer was a shrug of his shoulders. "Good enough for me."

"You were going to tell me what your plan is now that I somehow changed things," I said, bringing us back to the matter at hand.

"We want to join forces with Tricks and help expand the Hidden Empire, but with becoming his private army of sorts, we need his help in return," Eagle explained.

"Knew it couldn't be that straightforward," Weston grumbled.

"It's not really a deal if both parties don't get something out of it, you know," Sprocket pointed out.

I sighed and leaned back into Void, oddly comfortable in this giant's hold. "Wes, is there any coffee left? I didn't get to drink much of mine before I chucked it."

Much to my surprise, Cognac jumped to his feet and dashed towards the kitchen, shoving Wes back to his chair as he passed by. "No need, loverboy, I got this. She's our responsibility too for the next month. Guess you're gonna need to learn to share her."

Wes frowned at Cognac, then turned back to me. "What the hell does he mean, shortcake?"

"Little demon made a bet with me and lost, which means she agreed to stay with us for a month without trying to escape," Void answered, his voice rumbling against my back.

Cognac sauntered back into the room with a mug of steaming coffee, making sure that he brushed his fingers along mine as he handed it over. Glaring at him over the rim of my cup, I took a few gulps, letting the liquid burn down my throat.

"Clearly she didn't agree to the bet, seeing as she ran away with me hours ago," Wes snapped, arms crossed over his chest. "That, and it's obvious that you all seem to think you have a shot with Dax. What, are you all just going to fight over her until she picks someone?"

Eagle burst out laughing at Weston's words. "Good god, why would we make her pick?"

I couldn't help but perk up at what he was saying. I knew that something had changed with all the guys, but now it seemed I was going to learn what it was.

"We all agreed way beforehand that none of us alone would be enough for a woman. Our lifestyle doesn't come with normal hours or the ability to guarantee absolute safety, so having more than one partner to balance things out only makes sense. Could you say any different, Wester?" Eagle challenged.

Weston didn't answer right away; he just looked at each of the guys in turn, letting the silence hang. Then he leaned forward and rested his elbows on his knees.

"First of all, you guys have a lot to learn if you think Dax needs or wants anyone to protect or coddle her in life." He motioned towards me with a slight frown to his lips. "I'm not sure what voodoo magic you've worked on her over the past few days for her to look so relaxed and content in his hold, but that never happens. As for the second part of your argument, Dax and I have been together since I was twelve and she was ten. The longest we have ever gone not talking or seeing each other was the past two days. Hell, we even live together. There is nothing about this woman that I don't know. There is no competition between what you guys have to offer and I already do."

My jaw fell open at the word vomit that just fell out of Weston's mouth. He was never one to be a "Chatty Cathy" about our personal lives. Case in point—not many people knew we lived together, other than Harper, because she was my only normal friend. We didn't exactly interact with the most trustworthy people, being tied to Two Tricks.

"Oh, green is not a good color on you, Westilicious," Cognac snickered.

"There is no trick to this. My little demon just needs a firm hand before she will settle down," Void shared as he snuggled into me, his teeth scraping along my neck sending shivers straight to my clit.

How the fuck was I this turned on when Wes and I had just fucked like bunnies? These guys were bad for me in more ways than one.

Leaning back, I nuzzled into Void's neck until I latched onto his ear, biting down hard as I kicked my heel into his shin.

"Fucking hell, demon!" Void cried out as I slipped out of his hold and danced out of his reach when he went to grab for me.

I just blew a kiss to Void with a wink as he rubbed his ear with a pout on his lips.

"Sorry Voidykins, but it seems that we can't talk business if everyone keeps getting distracted by me." I shrugged. "Before someone else says or does anything asinine, why don't you tell me what it is you want in exchange for offering your services to Tricks?"

"We have to get rid of the only other roadblock and destroy the Mad Dogs MC before they really do attack us," Picasso answered. "Specifically, we need you, Dax, to do it to prove that if they mess with us, they mess with Two Tricks."

Chapter Twenty-Three
Eagle

I watched Dax's face go from her happy little smirk after teasing Void to slamming shut at Picasso's pronouncement. The look on her face alone told me that any chance we had to do this the way we wanted wasn't going to happen. My brother had just screwed the pooch because he had an overprotective little brother complex. Given the chance, I would have worked it in a way that would have made her choose to do the job, but now that we were telling her to do it, we didn't have a chance in hell.

"That's a tall order to ask when I haven't even told you I will bring it to Tricks. You guys ran Mastiff and his crew off years ago, what do you need Tricks' backing for?" Dax asked.

I knew my little hellcat wouldn't miss anything.

"Puzzler, Mastiff's father, was the president at the time, and he ran a disorganized crew. I decided because the boy was still so young it was wrong to kill him since he had a chance to get out of this life and start over. When we ran them out of town they lost everything, but instead of seeing it as a new start, he turned into one of the most ruthless leaders of the Mad Dogs, Nevada chapter. Mastiff has grown the Mad Dogs to three chapters big. If he really decides to come after us, then we will be wiped out for good, because he learned from my mistake and leaves no one alive," I explained, watching her bright blue eyes for any hint of what she was thinking.

Turning on her heel, she walked up the steps to the loft, leaving us sitting there with our thumbs up our asses. I glanced over at Weston to see if he had any clue what was going on, but he was sitting back in his chair with his head back and eyes closed.

If he wasn't worried, then I would leave her be for the moment, but it made my skin itch that she just walked away from me like that.

I'd been in my office, trying to get some work done when all the alarms went off and the security system on the fence went offline. It sent the whole compound into a panic —all the men knew of the danger we could be facing at any moment. Seeing the chaos reinforced to me that we needed to get stronger, smarter. And to do that, we needed people like Dax and Weston on our side. Two Tricks had the best of the best hidden in his empire, and I would do whatever it took to keep my people safe from a disaster I'd caused by being too weak.

"East, did you set off all the alarms and crash our system?" I asked, causing the man to open one eye at me, which he promptly closed.

My fists clenched at his disrespect. He might not be one of my crew, but he was someone I needed to get along with if I wanted Dax to stick around.

"My money's on you doing it because Dax isn't good

enough to infiltrate our system that fast. I had one of the best people I could find build the security for that, and he said the only one who was better than him worked exclusively for Tricks. Add in the fact that when we tried to look into Dax, there was absolutely no footprint for her anywhere on the web, and I think it was you," I pushed, hoping to get some kind of reaction out of him. Although, if he'd been living with Dax, that would be harder than I thought.

Weston sighed and opened his eyes, sitting up. "My consultation rate is three hundred an hour."

"Wessie, that is quite the pretty penny. How do we know you're worth it?" Cognac asked.

Clearly, Cognac had bonded with this guy in their time together, or he wouldn't be using those ridiculous nicknames. It had taken him years to stop doing that to the rest of us, but if you didn't get a nickname, then you were not on his good side.

"You're kidding, right? I literally demolished your security in five minutes from that crap computer and your cell phone. If I had my own setup, anything you had on your network would have been mine for the taking. Besides, that guy was right—I am one of the best," Weston answered, glaring at Cognac.

"So did your cocky-ass attitude rub off on her or did she rub off on you?" Sprocket asked, tapping his chin in thought. "Hmm, my guess is you got it from her. That woman came out of the womb ready to take over the world."

Seeing as how we finally got him talking, I was going to use it to my advantage. "The Phantom Saints would like to hire you to work on our system. We will pay your fee and buy whatever you tell us to so we can have the best system possible. I have women and children at the compound to think of and keep safe."

Footsteps thundered down the stairs as Dax came flying back into the room. "Oh, so you're willing to do whatever it takes to protect your people from this Mastiff jackass, no problem. Yet a guy who went to jail for you and ended up getting mixed up in a tough situation doesn't deserve your help? Explain the logic between that to me? He spent two fucking years in prison to keep you out so you could protect everyone else and keep the crew safe and running. Then, when you don't offer him any protection in jail, he does the best he can and then you just toss him out like trash!"

The venom in her words slapped me in the face, causing me to lean back as she stalked towards me. My mind raced, trying to catch up with where she was coming from... then I remembered. She had asked us a question when we first met her at the party. At that time we had no idea what she wanted from us, but we had obviously gotten it very wrong. I thought it was a metaphor for working with Tricks and what would happen if we betrayed him, not a literal scenario.

"Oh fuck. She asked you the question, didn't she?" Weston muttered, shaking his head.

I met Dax's gaze, her anger making her eyes more mesmerizing. "Ask me the question again."

She scoffed and balled her hands into fists, and my jaw started to ache again from her attention earlier.

"Dax—ask me the question again," I demanded.

Jutting out her chin, she took a deep breath and gave me the same scenario as last time, then asked me the question that meant more to her than she let on. "Upon him getting out of jail and coming back to the club, what would you do?"

"He never would have had to work with the drug ring in the first place because I would have had his back. Any man who would take the fall for me deserves to be protected in return. That man would have been welcomed back with open arms and a big-ass party," I answered, never letting my gaze waver from hers.

"Obviously you would change your answer—you knew you got it wrong last time. How can I believe anything you're saying now?" Dax demanded.

"Because that's what he did for me," Void answered.

Chapter Twenty-Four
Dax

It took me a moment to register what Void just said.

"Explain."

"Eight years ago, when we weren't as big of a crew as we are now, a guy named Lizard was kicked out of the club because he was pocketing money from drug deals he did. Pissed, he tried to get Eagle caught by setting us up with an undercover cop asking for black market weapons. Normally Eagle always takes the meeting with new people, but I had a bad feeling about it when he brought up knowing Lizard. I pulled my gun on him and got arrested before the deal could go any further. They wanted me to do ten years, but Gaby got it down to four, and I only did three because of good behavior," Void shared, his icy eyes never leaving mine. "While I was in, he made sure I had everything I needed, whether it was protection or a new toothbrush. Never once did I feel abandoned. Hell, he even sent Picasso to see me twice a month to keep me up to date on what was going on in the club."

The room was silent as they waited for me to react. I tried to hide how much I was reeling from this new information. My anger and hurt over what happened to my brother wanted me to push back at what he was saying, but I was too good at reading people to think it was all made up.

"Okay, so here's what I propose. Weston and I will join you at the compound so he can consult on your security. Meanwhile, I will look into Mastiff and the Mad Dogs to see if what you're asking me to do can even be done. If I think it's possible, then I will bring this all to Two Tricks and see what he has to say. Once he has made a choice, then and only then will I make good on our side of the bargain," I said, making sure to look at all of them as I spoke. "Oh, and you have to get this goddamn shock collar off of me or none of this is going to happen."

Eagle sat back and rubbed his chin, watching me with a critical eye. "So—you want to do this research on your own turf."

"I'm either truly your partner in this or the deal is off," I confirmed.

Picasso scoffed. "You want us to extend trust to you with no guarantee you will keep your word?"

"Sorry, did you miss the part where you will have Wes with you at the compound?" I asked. "We are both extending trust here."

"Hardly. He will be in our security systems; he could do whatever he wants to them to leave us vulnerable to an attack from Two Tricks," Picasso said, his face scrunched up in a scowl. "You have to leave the tracker on until Two Tricks agrees with the plan and we can talk to him face to face. That's when you can be free of it."

I growled at him, taking a step forward, but Wes reached out and grabbed my arm. "Take a moment to actually listen to what he is saying, Dax. It's a fair deal. You need to go back and show your face and deal with a few things before you can come back to the compound, and I can help you with your dead ends. It shouldn't take me more than three days to overhaul their whole system. If we need to order stuff in, then it could be longer, but I can still help you along the way."

My skin crawled at the thought of being tracked everywhere I went and them knowing where I lived. I wanted this thing off of me. The danger of being hit with that kind of shot at any given moment made me feel like this was a bigger leap of trust on my end.

"Fine. BUT if I end up getting shocked or the information you have on me gets out if the deal doesn't go your way, I will personally hand you over to the Mad Dogs and watch them kill you all. Do I make myself clear?" I snapped.

Eagle nodded, then got to his feet with his hand extended. I studied him for a moment, then took his hand, letting out a yelp as he pulled me forward and slammed his lips on mine. I fought the kiss at first, but then when his grip on my hip and neck felt like they might bruise, I relaxed into it.

When he finally released me, he grinned. "When Two Tricks agrees to the deal, make sure he knows that you will be spending a month living with us, so he'll have to deal with the commute time."

I scowled at him and shoved him off me. "There is no telling what Tricks will think of this deal. It's going against one of his rules, and he doesn't like it when things fuck with his rules."

I felt someone step up behind me, molding his chest to my back. "Don't sell yourself short there, little rebel," Sprocket said, his lips brushing the shell of my ear. "That silver tongue of yours could talk anyone into doing something they didn't plan on."

Something about all these men turned my abnormally high libido into overdrive as my body sang with desire. I glanced out of the corner of my eye at Sprocket, knowing he was trying to do the exact thing he just suggested about me. Leaning into him, I reached up and let my hand sink into his hair that was piled up in a messy bun. He almost seemed to purr at the attention, but just as I was going to get a nice grip on his hair, he grabbed my waist and yanked me away from him as if it was as simple as a dance.

"Oh little rebel, haven't you learned? Your tricks don't work on me," Sprocket teased, his eyes shining with mirth. "You're going to have to up your game if you want to play with me."

Shaking him off, I headed for the door of the cabin. "Well, let's get this show on the road. I'll drive the ATV back to the compound and then I'll take my Camaro back home."

"Looks like Cognac gets to ride bitch to one of us," Void chuckled as they followed me out the door.

"Wait, you can't leave the place like this!" Eagle called out, still in the living room.

I looked at Void, who was on my right, and shook my head. "I've never met a man who could be more of a neat freak than Weston."

"You get used to it. Else you end up with a black eye or your hand stabbed with the fork you left in the sink," Void said with a shrug.

Pausing, I hollered back through the open door. "This safehouse is burned now that you guys know about it. Tricks will probably just sell the place or burn it down, one of the two depending on his mood. So there's no point in worrying about it."

Boots clomped to the door, and Eagle glared down at me, holding out his hand. "Then I'll buy it off him right now. Hand over the keys, this place is the perfect getaway."

"Yeah, no can do, pres. We have to have a crew come and wipe the place of all our stash and security," I said as I skipped down the steps to the ATV.

Eagle snarled, giving the place one more lookover and forcing himself to walk out the door, Picasso right on his heels.

"You have to hand it to the guy—he has a great operation. There is no way you guys would have found the place if it hadn't been for the GPS," Cognac mused while taking in the forest around us. "Hey, when you talk to Two Tricks about the deal, tell him we will pay market price for this place. I wouldn't mind spending a weekend out here sometime."

I rolled my eyes at him, which caused his grin to grow wider. "You guys keep forgetting I have to check out if going after the Mad Dogs is the right move or not. I actually like staying alive, and I'd like to keep doing that for a while longer."

"Come on, Cognac. You can ride with me," Sprocket said, slapping his friend on the back.

Void and Picasso followed after them while Eagle watched Wes lock the place up and toss me the keys.

"You know what, I think you should come with me, little hellcat. I don't trust that you won't drive off with the two of you in the buggy. Tech wiz over here knows there's a tracker, and if he's as good as he claims, he could disable that in no time," Eagle decided.

"Nah, I'm good going back with Wes. I'm not a girl who

rides bitch when she has the option to drive," I said, turning to hop in the ATV.

Big arms grabbed me around the waist and tossed me over a shoulder.

"What the fuck is it with you assholes and dragging me around like a sack of potatoes! Put me down right now, Eagle, or I swear to god I will make you crash your bike!" I yelled, punching hard against his lower back, trying to hit his kidney.

A hand smacked against my ass, the sound of it echoing through the trees. "Watch what you say. I already owe you punishment for leaving my room a mess, don't make me add to it."

Ignoring his warning, I wiggled around, grabbing his boxers to try and give him a wedgie from hell when two more hits on my ass in quick succession left a burn on my skin, which stopped me.

"I can do this all day, it's up to you when I stop," Eagle commented as he continued on his way back to his bike.

I pushed up to see Wes standing by the ATV, eyes wide in shock and trying not to laugh. *Oh, that fucker was going to pay for not helping me. See if he gets as much as a hand job from me any time soon, the unhelpful bastard.* We broke through the trees onto a small side road that was more well used and wasn't as rough as the one leading to the cabin. Pulling me off his shoulder, Eagle dropped me unceremoniously onto the ground, causing me to sputter as I got to my feet.

"Are you trying to do everything in your power to piss me the fuck off? Because if you are, you're doing a great job!" I fumed.

Eagle rounded on me, grabbing me once again by the throat. "It seems that there has been a slight miscommunication in all this. You might work for Two Tricks, but you are ours. The Phantom Saints leadership has claimed you. So yeah, I'm fucking pissed that I'm going to bring you back home and then you're going to get in your car and leave for who the fuck knows how long. I won't know what you're doing, if you're eating, if you're drinking too much, or getting into trouble!"

Bewildered, I gaped at Eagle, trying to understand what he just said. Then anger washed over me in a tidal wave as his words hit home. How the fuck did they get it into their heads that I was theirs, of all things? I didn't remember signing up for that job.

Roaring at him, I reached out and grabbed his throat, gripping it far tighter than he was mine. "I. Belong. To. No one! I told you from day one that I was not part of your crew. My loyalties are to myself and no one else. I will not be forced into this, because you made the decision without even TELLING me! This woman cannot be bought or sold like a piece of meat, so get that thought out of your goddamn head this instant."

We both glared at each other, everyone around us completely silent as they watched to see what would happen next. A flash of pride shown in Eagle's eyes before he removed his hand from my neck. When I felt confident that he wasn't going to make another move against me, I pulled my hand away, seeing a perfect impression of my hand on his throat with little crescent moons from my nails biting in.

"We will talk about this later," Eagle said, walking over to his bike.

I let out a huff, amazed at the sheer hard-headedness of this man. "I'm not riding back with you. Pick someone else."

"Fine, you'll ride with Picasso then," he answered without even looking back at me.

I narrowed my eyes, feeling like that was far too easy of a compromise. Turning, I looked at Picasso as he frowned at his brother's back, then shifted to me. Jerking his head for me to get on, I took a deep breath and swung my leg over the seat. Once comfortable, I grabbed onto the belt loops on his hips, not feeling welcome to wrap my arms around his waist. Oddly, I felt more comfortable sitting bitch for someone who didn't actually care for me all that much.

I couldn't place my finger on why, but the man who made me an egg in a hole hadn't shown up since. He was far more closed off and untrusting. It couldn't just be the whole brother complex thing, because other than today, I hadn't truly meant harm to Eagle. The man was an artist, and I knew from personal experience that we were all fickle bitches. He either needed to get laid or spend the day locked in his art space for a day to get whatever had crawled up his ass to mellow the fuck out.

Chapter Twenty-Five
Picasso

The feeling of Dax's chest glued to my back as we drove back to the compound made my skin tingle at the contact. This spitfire of a woman was wreaking havoc in my world, and I loved it and hated it, all at the same time. I was the only one out of the leadership that hadn't ever had a serious relationship before. My brother and the Phantom Saints were my top priority in the world, and no one had given me a reason to change my thinking. That is, until this tornado landed in our house, tossing everything into chaos. She didn't care about our carefully laid out rules and the way we did things. Nope, she did what she wanted, damn the consequences.

I thought for sure Eagle would kill her the first time he found her in his room, soaking in his bathtub, no less. The last thing I expected was to hear the sounds of Dax screaming out in pleasure instead of pain. Seeing how fast everyone else was becoming enamored with this spitfire, I knew I needed to figure out who she really was, so I volunteered to keep an eye on her that first day. That had wholeheartedly been a mistake. Now I craved her touch, her attention, anything to get those silvery-blue eyes to look at me.

So what did I do? I pushed her away, of course.

Hearing her reject our claim on her made me feel more confident in keeping her at arm's length. Our family was known to fall hard and fast when we decided on someone, and it was already happening with Eagle. Out of the group, one of us needed to keep a level head and remember the big picture.

If we were going to survive against the Mad Dogs, we needed Two Tricks' help, and if he wasn't willing to give it then we would just have to take it from him. I was a little less certain that Dax would be swayed to our side after the confrontation that just happened, but there was no telling if she would change her mind or not. We couldn't leave this to chance—it was too important.

Pulling into the compound, I drove right up to the house and parked beside the garage that I had turned into my room/studio. Dax popped off my bike before I could even put the kickstand down, hands on her hips as she watched the others park their bikes in the large garage attached to the clubhouse.

"I thought you said you had a whole group of your guys waiting off a little ways in case you needed backup," Dax called, cocking a hip in irritation.

Eagle just grinned at her, pleased that she noticed it was a lie after she believed him. "Good thing I didn't need them in the long run."

"God, I can't wait to get out of here and back to my normal life," Dax sighed, turning on her heel and marching up the steps.

Eagle's face turned into a storm cloud of anger at her words. He moved to charge after her, but I stepped in front of him, bringing him to a halt.

"Eagle, if you want her to ever come back, you need to ease back just a bit," I said, putting a hand on his shoulder and giving it a squeeze. "She is a spitfire who doesn't like to be caged, and that's all we represent to her right now."

My brother looked at me with a cocked eyebrow. "What's this? Have you finally taken the stick out of your ass about her?"

Frowning, I shoved him back as he laughed at me. "Fuck you, Eagle. One of us has to keep an eye on the prize."

"Oh, no need for you to worry about that—I've got both trained on her ass at all times," Cognac said as he walked past us.

"I'm surrounded by idiots," I groaned.

"Yeah, I'm gonna need you not to lump me in with this sorry-ass crew of idiots. I have no problem thinking with my brain and not my dick, thank you very much," Sprocket pointed out, joining our conversation. "Those two dipshits are in a league of their own, though," he added, nodding his head at Cognac and Void, who were shoving each other out of the way to get in the house first.

"Truthfully though, we should all be impressed that she got Void of all people to show a soft side. He doesn't typically do anything sweet or gentle—I mean, he won't even fuck a woman in the pussy because he wants to make sure they don't get pregnant on him," Eagle shared.

I scrunched my face up and shook my head, not really wanting to picture Void fucking. "Why the fuck do you even know that?" I asked but held up a hand when he went to answer. "Nevermind, I don't want to know."

"So what's the real plan?" Sprocket asked, pulling our attention from the house.

"I'm going back with her," I blurted out.

"Really..." Eagle said, brows creased.

I rubbed my shoulder where the Saints symbol was tattooed, knowing this was the right move. "Look, even with the tracker on her, we have no idea what she is really doing. We are taking a big risk letting Westy work on our system. Think about it—we have him here and I go with her, each holding the other accountable. He means a lot to her, probably her one weakness, and I'm the same for you. It's a fair trade."

"I'm not the one you need to convince there, Picasso—she is. If she'll take you, then I won't stop you, but this might not go the way you think it should. What are you going to do if she says 'fuck off, no deal at all'?" Eagle asked.

"Like I said, we have the one person who is her weakness, and if she has to hate me forever, then I am willing to take that burden so our people will be safe. She isn't more important than the two hundred people we are protecting," I answered.

"Fuck. And they say I'm the cold-hearted bastard out of the two of us. Alright, I'll back you on this, but just know that if we lose the deal and have no protection for our people, that's on you," Eagle stated, giving me a nod before heading off to the house.

Sprocket stepped in front of me, forcing me to look him in the eye. "Explain your reasoning to her just like you did to Eagle. Under all the walls she has built up, protecting people close to her is something that is important to her and that she respects in others. The question she asked was to gauge our loyalty to our members—somewhere along the way, someone wasn't loyal to her or one of her people, and it cost them in a way she couldn't forgive. Let down the wall of ice for her to get how much this means to you and the lengths you'll go, and she will give in."

As he walked back to the house, what he said hit home. He was right—the way she protected Weston was exactly what I'd done for Eagle. The loyalty that people had to her wasn't just because they were scared of her, but also because she kept them safe. Any neighborhood the Hidden Empire controlled had significantly less crime, and businesses thrived. Thinking back to our conversation at the cabin, I realized it wasn't until after Void told his story that she'd been willing to talk to Two Tricks. We had been going about this the wrong way the whole time.

Now armed with this information, it was time to put it into action. I wasn't going to let her leave the compound without me, come hell or high water.

Chapter Twenty-Six
Dax

I showed Wes the room that I'd been staying in, figuring that's where they would have him sleep. The other guys stayed downstairs, hanging out in the living room like nothing unusual had happened today.

"Is there anything in here that you want to take back with you?" Wes asked as he looked around for anything that showed I had even been here.

"Eagle eye hates messes, so if I leave anything out, he seems to pick it up and put it away. Truthfully, I didn't think there was anyone that could be worse than you when it came to being a neat freak. I wonder what he did with the mess I left in his room through," I rambled, then shrugged my shoulders. "Do we need to go get your bike? I don't suppose you packed for a few days' stay in a biker gang's compound. Seems like I will have to bring you back some stuff if you really plan on doing this."

Wes just sat on the bed and watched me as I paced the room. "My bike is stashed somewhere safe. I'm sure I can get one of the guys to take me to it. As for the clothes, I would be grateful for you to bring me back some."

I nodded absently, continuing my pacing and started plucking at my bottom lip. Wes grabbed my arm and pulled me into a hug, trapping my hands against his chest.

"Talk to me, shortcake," Wes said into my ear. "It's me and you until the end. No matter what you decide to do, I will support you one hundred percent."

Deciding to give into the support he was offering, I snuggled into his hold and rested my head under his chin. "If Devin had been a part of this crew, do you think he would still be alive?"

Hearing Void's story made all the feelings about my brother come rushing back. They had been locked away for so many years that I believed I was over it, but clearly that wasn't the case.

"There's no way to know that. Devin was never as street smart as you are. He trusted people too easily and was talked into all kinds of situations that could have gotten him into trouble. It's not your fault either because you weren't there. He still would have married Kimber and ended up in the Blackjax. I will say the same thing I have said for years—not every MC is the same. You've spent time here—are they what you thought they would be?" Wes challenged.

"Why do you care so much that I change my mind about MCs?" I questioned.

Wes pulled me back so he could look me in the eyes. "I don't give a shit about how you feel about MCs. What I care about is you. The anger you have focused on them isn't healthy, and if you don't eventually let it go, it will eat you alive. Believe it or not, you've changed in the short time you've been here. Something inside of you has softened." Catching my expression, he explained further. "I don't mean weak—you could never be weak. You've let them get a glimpse of who you are, the side of Dax that only Harper and I have seen."

"Now you're just spouting a bunch of bullshit," I said, shoving him back and heading for the door. "I'll make sure to get you clothes tomorrow. I'd share mine, but I don't think they will fit."

"Very funny. I'll see if the guys can loan me some sweatpants or something. If they can pay my fee, I'm sure they can figure something out," Wes said, chuckling as we headed back downstairs.

"Yo, Eagle, I'm gonna need my cell phone back. And my car keys," I called once I caught sight of him at the pool table.

Eagle smirked at me and nodded his head in Picasso's direction. "Sure thing. He's got them for you already."

I walked over to Picasso and noticed the saddle bags that were at his feet. "Going on a trip?"

"Yeah, back to your place." He looked me dead in the eye, waiting for me to challenge him.

I tossed my head back and laughed. "You must be outta your goddamn mind if you think I'm letting you, the asshole who shocked me, come with."

"Think about it. Weston is staying here to work on our system. If I go with you, it keeps things fair."

"Nope, sorry, that still isn't gonna do it for me. Try again," I snapped, crossing my arms.

Picasso sighed, running his hands through his hair. "Look, I know you don't think very highly of us MCs, but the threat to all the people living here is real. My job as a leader of this crew is to make sure I do whatever it takes to keep them safe. Our members have wives and kids that don't deserve to live in fear. How can I look them in the eye if I don't do everything possible to keep them safe?"

His words were a slap in the face, and I couldn't help but be impressed with this side of him.

"You can come on two conditions—one, Weston has to agree to you coming to our house, and two, you are not going to meet with Two Tricks. I will deal with that matter on my own, along with whatever other business I need to handle as enforcer."

"If someone can spot me clothes for tomorrow until Dax comes back with some for me, then I'm cool with it," Wes said. "You're letting me stay in your home, it's only fair that I do the same. After all, we are hoping for a partnership, right?" Wes added, grinning at me.

God, he could be such a smug bastard sometimes.

"Ready?" I asked, holding out my hand for my things, which he gave me right away.

"Yup, let me show you where we stashed your ride," Picasso said, hoisting his saddle bags over his shoulder.

I followed him out the door until I was dragged back by Weston, of all people. "Did you really think you could just leave without saying goodbye?"

Confused, I just scrunched my face at him. "Bye?"

Weston cupped my face, tilting my head up, and gave me a kiss so intense I was breathless when he let me come up for air. "See you later, shortcake."

A grin tugged at my lips as Eagle shoved Weston out of the way and came in for his own goodbye kiss. "Keep each other safe, you hear me?"

"I'll make sure Picasso is the safest person in L.A. as long as Weston is looked after as well," I countered.

"What matters to you, little hellcat, matters to me. He'll be fine," Eagle said, his thumb brushing my cheek. "Be back for dinner tomorrow. We are having a cookout to celebrate our new friendship."

"Tricks hasn't agreed yet, Eagle. Don't go putting all your bullets in one gun," I warned.

Eagle just smiled at me, then gave Picasso a bro hug as the other three came to say goodbye.

"Seriously, guys, I'm just leaving for the day—apparently I need to be back for dinner. There's no need to get all sappy about it." I groaned when Cognac scooped me up in a hug and twirled me around like a kid, then gave me a peck on the lips.

"Where's the fun in that? I like watching you squirm under all this attention—makes you seem more girly," Cognac teased, dodging my punch.

Sprocket gave me a side hug and kissed me on the forehead with a wink. "Don't have too much fun without us."

"No fear of that. I have old stick-in-the-mud coming with me," I said, gesturing to Picasso.

"Hey! I know how to have fun," he grumbled.

"I'll believe it when I see it, buddy." I smirked then let out a squeak when someone bit the shell of my ear.

Looking up, I saw Void standing behind me with his hands resting on my hips. "Little demon, if you think you can run from us because we are giving you some freedom, that would be a mistake. I will hunt you down no matter where you hide, no matter how long it takes."

A shiver of pleasure went up my spine at the intensity in his voice and eyes. There was no doubt in my mind he would indeed come through on that promise.

"Noted, big guy," I said with a wink, pulling away from him. "Someday I might have to test that, though—you never know what life will bring in this dark world we share."

"Come on, let's get out of here before they change their

minds and lock you away in the bedroom," Picasso muttered, heading out.

I gave the guys a girly finger wave and blew a kiss before skipping down the steps of the house. Picasso led me to a small one-and-a-half car garage off to the side of the clubhouse and entered in the code to the keypad. The door lifted, and there was my beautiful baby, the fading sunlight filling the garage with a pink glow.

Running a hand along the hood, I unlocked the door and slid into the front seat. Pushing the start button, the Camaro purred to life, the throaty exhaust music to my ears. After days of being unable to go anywhere I wanted, this was pure bliss. Pulling out of the garage, I found Picasso on his bike, ready and waiting for me. I took a moment to sync up my phone and cranked up the volume as Halestorm's *Love Bites (So Do I)* blasted through the sound system.

Let's see what kind of fun Picasso can have.

I drove at a normal pace out of the compound, seeing as the driveway wasn't super smooth, but once we hit pavement, I gunned it. The engine roared to life, and I was off like a shot, whooping my joy as I ate up the miles.

The familiar growl of a motorcycle came from behind, letting me know Picasso was up for the challenge. With the sun setting, the sky was cast in warm tones of orange, pink, and yellow, setting the stage for a great drive. Rolling down the windows, I let the warm breeze flow through the car. My bliss was short-lived, though, as my phone started sounding, loading all the missed messages, calls, and notifications from the past few days.

Knowing that most of them would be from Harper, I decided the best thing to do was to just call her back. Rolling up the windows and killing the music, I hit her speed dial, and one ring later, she answered.

"You better have died for you to fall off the planet like that, missy!" Harper screeched. "Do you know how worried I was? Weston wouldn't even tell me what happened, no matter how much I begged. I got my first gray hair from you, I'll have you know! Expect a bill from me for the hair salon to fix what you did to me!"

Rolling my eyes, I leaned back as she continued to rant about how I was the world's worst friend and so on. Fifteen minutes later, when she had ranted herself out, I knew it was safe to try and talk.

"Hi Harper, how are you? The past few days have been hell for me, but let's not focus on that. I'll finally be home tonight, if you want to catch up?"

At this, Harper started to laugh like she was the Wicked Witch of the West. "Dax Rose Blackmore, there not a snowball's chance in hell you are getting away without giving me some kind of explanation."

I grinned as an idea came to me. "If you want to come over, I will explain everything to you until you're satisfied. Sound fair?"

"I'll be there in ten minutes," Harper said, and the call was cut off.

Should I call her back and tell her that I was still thirty minutes away? Nah, she'd figure it out.

Chapter Twenty-Seven
Dax

Pulling up to the house, I saw Harper's cute little red Fiat parked along the street. I smirked as I saw her sitting on the steps to the front door, her lips turned down in a deep frown. I left the door open as Picasso pulled in after me, and I motioned him to put his bike inside.

Seconds later, Harper was all up in my face. "You could have told me that you were going to take that long! Seriously, how inconsiderate can you be, Dax?"

"I was going to tell you, but you hung up before I could say anything," I defended.

"Ha! You could have texted me, or hell, even called me back to share that tidbit of info. Why do you hate me?" Harper pouted, actual tears welling up in her eyes.

She knew that the one thing I could never win against was her crying. "No, nope, none of that," I said pointing my finger at her eyes. "This is not serious enough for you to use that on me. This isn't the first time I've been gone for a few days."

Harper sniffled a few times and used her knuckle to wipe under her eyes, then froze, her eyes widening in surprise. I'd forgotten about Picasso with all her theatrics. Miracle of miracles, her tears dried up, and she was shaking out her hair and checking how many buttons she had open on her button-down silk blouse. Shaking my head at her, I half-turned so she could get a better look at him.

"Oh, hello, Dax didn't mention she had someone with her," Harper said, giving me a glare and holding her hand out to Picasso. "I'm Harper, Dax's best friend."

He took her manicured hand and shook it gently, looking very out of place with the whole interaction. "Picasso."

"This is the reason I have been MIA the last few days. We met at the party, and we hit it off so well I went to spend some time with him at his house." I smiled as I snaked my arm around his waist and slid my hand up under his shirt so my palm was resting on his stomach. "With how crazy things got, I didn't know where you got to, and I let Weston know not to worry but realized I didn't give him much to go on other than I was alright. You know how it can get when you're swept away in the passion of things."

Picasso froze under my touch, but as I talked, he relaxed and let his arm rest over my shoulders, pulling me closer to him. "She begged me to come back with her since she didn't want to leave but she already canceled a few days of clients. I just couldn't let her abandon everything to stay with me."

Look at this cheeky asshole, making it sound like I'm the desperate one. Game on, my friend. Game on.

"Well, since your brother had to go back to work, it just isn't the same without both of you involved, you know. It seems I have a sex drive that can wear out two badass biker dudes. Lucky for them, they had some friends who were down to play when they needed naps," I said, patting his stomach before I started walking for the front door, leaving him gaping at me.

Harper was right on my heels. "You're telling me that you went missing for a three-day sexcipade?!"

"You told me that I needed to let loose and get some." I shrugged as I unlocked the door, letting us all into the house. "I'm sorry, did you want to join us?" I asked as I hung my keys on the hook in the kitchen.

"I love you girl, but no. I don't think we will ever be at the level to do something like that," Harper said, smirking at me. "So where are the other friends that were involved? Are they all that hot?" she whispered as I grabbed a beer out of the fridge.

I leaned in, seeing Picasso taking in the house. "Hotter."

Harper groaned and flopped down on the barstool, head down on the counter. "Why don't these things happen to me???"

"Guess you just need to keep trying, babe. I never expected to be all but kidnapped by five men at a party," I consoled, rubbing her back. "So how do we feel about pizza and wings? Weston is gone for a few days on a consulting job and we all know I'm banned from the kitchen."

"Sounds perfect, but I'm going to steal a shirt because I can't risk getting grease on this fabric," Harper said, heading upstairs. "Order us the usual, k' babe?"

While Harper went to raid my room, I headed straight for Picasso. "You will not utter one word about Two Tricks, the Hidden Empire, our deal, or that you are with the Phantom Saints, am I clear? She knows nothing about that part of my life, and I plan to keep it that way."

"Let me guess—you also want me to play along with this

story you made up about us too," Picasso said, grabbing the beer out of my hand and taking a long pull from the bottle.

I nodded yes.

"Fine, but just know that you are the one who came up with the story, not me."

Scowling at him, I went back to the kitchen to grab another beer and dialed our favorite pizza place.

"Thank you for calling Lucifer's Pizza, my name is Beth, how can I help you?"

"Hey Beth, it's Dax," I answered.

"Oh, hey girl! Are we doing the usual with wings or without?"

"With wings, but we are going to need the version for three people," I said, trying to keep my voice down, seeing that Picasso was looking at me with raised eyebrows.

"You got it girl. We are delivering that to the same place, right?"

"Yup."

"Alright, I got that all set for you, and we will put it on the tab. Should be to you guys in like twenty minutes!"

"Thanks Beth. Have a good night," I said, hanging up.

"Eagle would have a fit if he knew that you ordered out enough to be on a first-name basis with the employees and have a 'usual,'" Picasso laughed.

Rolling my eyes, I waved for him to follow me past the kitchen into the family room, or as we called it, "the cave." It was painted a dark gray, setting off the stark white wall that the projector showed on. There were three recliners on a platform along the back wall and a large couch that was almost as deep as a bed. Pillows and blankets were scattered over the lower couch, making it a cozy nest to curl up in. Cupholders were cut into the fabric near the back of the couch for convenience.

"What the hell is this?" Picasso asked as he took in the room. "Is that a popcorn machine?"

I grinned at him as I crawled onto the couch. "You didn't think we would just eat microwave popcorn like heathens, did you?"

"You can't cook in the kitchen but you can use that thing to make popcorn?" Picasso questioned.

"No, I'm the one who makes the popcorn," Harper shared, entering the room in a pair of my shorts and a t-shirt, which meant they turned into booty shorts and a crop top. "She will smoke us out of here if she touches that thing. This is the third one they've bought because she killed the other two."

I watched Picasso as Harper made her way to the mini-fridge where her girly drinks were kept, but he didn't follow her movements. Instead, he walked over to the built-in bookcases filled with hundreds of movies and TV shows. Trying to stifle my grin, I took a pull from my beer as Harper took her spot in the corner with her favorite blanket.

"What should we watch tonight?" I asked, knowing the battle that was about to begin.

Harper popped up and grabbed the notebook off the counter. "Let's see, you picked the first movie last time, which was *Alien vs. Predator*, and my pick was *Sleepless in Seattle*. Guess that means I get to pick first this time!"

"Do I get a say in what we watch?" Picasso interjected.

"Actually, I don't know—there's never been a guest over for a pizza and movie night," Harper said, tapping her painted nail on her chin. "I guess we just do what we do when Weston joins us."

"What is that, exactly?" Picasso asked.

I rolled off the couch and walked over to a cabinet,

opening the doors to reveal a dartboard. "The first person to get a bullseye gets to pick the movie."

A wide smile grew on Picasso's face. "Now this I can get behind! Alright, I'll go first since this is your home turf and you have the advantage."

"How about I even give you one extra throw to even it out?" I offered.

Harper paused and looked at me with a shocked expression. I just frowned at her and handed two darts to Picasso. Showing him where to stand, I stepped back and waited as he settled in for his first throw. After a moment, he sent the dart sailing down the length of the room, and it hit just outside the bullseye. Shifting a little, he threw the second, hitting dead center.

"Wait, he didn't play the right way though," Harper interjected.

"Different rules for this situation, babe," I said, flinging my dart over my shoulder as I walked back to the couch.

"The fuck?!" Picasso blurted, letting me know it had indeed also hit the bullseye. "How do you normally play?"

"Depends on how heated the argument or how badly the other wants to win, but they're always blindfolded. Sometimes they spin each other around or do some other crazy thing to throw them off their game," Harper said as she plucked her movie off the shelf, ignoring the fish impression Picasso was doing. "Alright, we're gonna start the night off with *Crazy Rich Asians*!"

Picasso leaned down until I could feel the heat of his breath on my skin. "Does she always pick chick movies?"

"Every single time. But she's taking pity on you—this isn't as bad as you think. It's actually kinda funny," I whispered back. "Now go pick what you want to watch."

Harper danced over to the DVD player, and I got everything turned on and cued up for us when the sound of the doorbell echoed in the room.

"I'll grab it, it's probably the pizza," I called as I headed for the front door.

Glancing at the security feed that popped up on my phone, I saw that it was indeed the pizza, but it was a new driver. Tino was typically who they sent to our place, knowing that we didn't like just anyone coming to the house. Lucifer's was one of the businesses that hired us for protection, so they knew who I was and who I worked for. Weston and I had worked out a deal with the owner to make sure only vetted staff knew our address.

I paused and walked over to the closet, where I had a single handgun safe bolted to the wall. Placing my hand on it so it could scan my palm, the safe popped open, and I grabbed the gun. Walking slowly to the door, I watched the guy holding the insulated delivery bag, but his head was down and he wasn't looking around or getting impatient at the wait. Nothing about this sat right with me. Clicking the intercom on, I listened for a moment, but the man's breathing was calm and steady.

"Hey, thanks for the delivery. Could you leave it at the door? I've got my hands full dealing with a sick pet," I said into the intercom.

The man shifted and opened the bag and set the food off to the side, but what also spilled out was a handgun. Quick as I could while he was bent over, I tossed the locks and yanked the door open, hitting the guy over the head with the butt of my gun. He dropped to the ground, thankfully not on top of our food. Shoving my gun into the back of my waistband, I grabbed the food and brought it to the cave, making sure I didn't show off my back.

"Pizza! Hey, let me go grab some plates and stuff out of

the kitchen, I'll be right back," I said as I backed out of the room again, rushing to the front door.

Grabbing the man under his armpits, I pulled him into the house and over to the garage door. Once in the garage, I pushed a set of shelves to the side, revealing a hidden door to the basement. Hoisting the stranger up, I dragged him down the stairs, his feet thudding on the steps as we went. Bless Weston for making sure we did soundproofing through the whole thing. Reaching the bottom of the stairs, I heaved the man into the metal chair that was bolted to the concrete floor and strapped him in. I plucked one of the gags off the wall, wanting to make extra sure that my guests wouldn't know this man was down here if he decided to wake up screaming in the dark.

"God, it's good to be home," I sighed as I jogged back up the steps and covered the entrance. I grabbed two fresh beers, plates, and everything else we needed before heading back to the cave.

"What did you pick out, Picasso?" I asked, setting things down as if I didn't just tie a man up in my basement.

"*Windtalkers*. I've never seen it, but I heard it's a good movie," Picasso said as we all got comfy to watch Harper's choice first.

Chapter Twenty-Eight
Dax

"I warned you the Ringburner wasn't a joke," I teased as Picasso glared at me when he came back from the bathroom.

"It wasn't that spicy to eat, how was I supposed to know the exit was gonna be worse?" he grumbled.

Harper and I just laughed as we picked up before heading into the kitchen.

"Ah, I forget how much fun it is the first time someone eats that pizza," Harper sighed, a smile on her lips. "The sauce on the wings was extra in the best way tonight, too."

"Do you two even have a stomach lining left after eating shit like that?" Picasso asked.

Sticking out my bottom lip, I walked up and rubbed his stomach. "Poor baby, was it too much for you to handle?"

He batted my hand away and frowned down at me. "Only a demon like you would enjoy something that fucking spicy. You could have at least warned me before I ate one."

Grinning, I divided the leftover wings and gave half to Harper as she grabbed her stuff to head out.

"Thanks for making time for me in your sex-filled life," Harper said, then winked at Picasso. "Hopefully I'll get to meet his brother and friends sometime soon."

"You never know." I shrugged, walking her to the front door. "Stranger things have happened."

As I opened it, I noticed the delivery guy's gun was still on the stoop, so I walked out with her to her car, making sure she didn't notice it. Harper was my one pure goodness that I allowed in my life, and I wanted to do everything in my power to keep it that way.

"Talk to you soon, love ya babe," Harper said, blowing me a kiss as she got in her car.

Waving, I headed back to the house, wracking my brain as I tried to figure out how I was going to deal with the stranger in my basement. It was too coincidental that the night I got home with one of the Phantom Saints, an armed stranger showed up at my door. This needed to be handled without Picasso knowing until I could figure out what I was dealing with. Finding him in the kitchen putting the dishes in the dishwasher, I couldn't help but smile. His brother has trained him so well he just couldn't help himself

"Come on, let me show you where you're sleeping," I called, waving for him to follow.

I brought him all the way up to my floor and stopped at the little living room that I had. Walking over to the couch, I pulled off the cushions and pushed the coffee table out of the way. Seeing what I was up to, Picasso grabbed the handle for the bed and pulled it out. It was brand new—no one had ever slept on it before—so I had no idea if it was comfortable or not. I headed for the closet in my art room where I kept the extra sheets I bought for it. When I turned around, I almost crashed into him as he stood, taking in my studio.

"You did all this?" he whispered, walking up to the piece I had been working on before I got kidnapped.

"Nope, I just rent the space for someone else to use right outside my bedroom door," I deadpanned.

Ignoring my passive-aggressive comment, he moved deeper into the room, where my finished pieces were stacked. I was supposed to drop off new work for the art gallery and just hadn't gotten to it yet. Picasso flipped through the paintings until he stopped and pulled one out, holding it up.

The painting was of a woman who had clearly just had sex but was left alone in the bed. Curled into a ball, arms wrapped around the pillow and the sheet barely covering her ass, a tear shimmered on her cheek.

The same emotions I'd been feeling as I painted that came rushing back. This was why I didn't want anyone to know that I was the artist. Raw emotions were bled over every canvas; it was the one place I allowed myself to feel everything. Now having Picasso, a fellow artist, seeing into my soul, it was too much.

Leaving the room, I set to work on getting the bed made, refusing to let the tears that welled in my eyes fall. I was stronger than this; I didn't need anyone to coddle me and tell me everything would be alright. We could survive without romance. Physical need was just that—a need. There didn't need to be emotion to scratch an itch and move on with your life. It was the world and society that said everyone needed to have a special person that you connected with romantically. For the life of me, I couldn't figure out why. All it did was make things complicated and messy. I didn't have time for that kind of shit in my life.

As I tucked in the last corner of the sheet, I went to grab pillows from my room when Picasso's arms wrapped around my waist, pulling me to his chest. "So the little vixen has a soft side."

He leaned down and brushed his nose along the shell of my ear, sending a shiver down my back. "Tonight you showed me the person who painted those pieces. Harper makes you vulnerable in ways I haven't even seen around Weston. So tell me, which one is the real Dax?"

Turning in his arms, I looked up at him, his chocolate-colored eyes filled with desire and fear.

"They both are, but the Dax that Harper sees died a long time ago with her twin. Harper is the only person that I still know and keep in contact with from that time of my life. That was back when I still had rose-colored glasses and thought I would travel the world with my paints. Seems the universe had different plans for me and decided to teach me the hard way that the world will take everything from you unless you fight to keep it safe. I won't risk that happening again, Picasso, no matter what it costs me to do it."

"Don't you get it, Dax? We are the same in this. We need to fight together, not against one another. The woman who can paint like that is just as strong as the enforcer for an underlord. Not everything needs to come with bloodshed and brutality." Picasso's voice was raw with the emotions he was feeling.

I stood there searching his face, trying to see what he saw in me to say something so very innocent. He still had his whole family. They might not agree with what he was doing with his life, but they were still alive to care. There was no way he could know the pain of losing the other half of your soul. Weston and Harper helped me patch what heart I had left together, but it was scarred and tainted. The things I'd done to keep my people safe would leave anyone blemished, and it wasn't going to end any time soon.

"It's pretty to think that, Picasso, but that isn't the world I live in, and one of these days you'll have to take your own blindfold off and see it isn't yours either. Thinking that people won't do whatever it takes to survive will get you killed. I can't protect you from yourself—no one can," I whispered and pulled out of his arms.

I walked into my room, grabbed two of the forty pillows I had, and brought them back to him. "I'm going to work on a few things down in Weston's office. If you need anything, just make yourself at home."

Picasso opened his mouth as if he was going to say something more but then thought better of it.

After an hour or so catching up on emails and things for Silver Bullet Ink, I decided it was time to deal with my surprise houseguest. I stopped at the landing to listen, but the house was silent, making me feel fairly confident Picasso was asleep. Glancing at the clock in the kitchen, I saw it was one a.m., and from what I noticed, these boys were early to bed, early to rise, so it seemed a safe bet.

Back out in the garage, I shifted the shelves and flicked on the light as I headed down. With each step, I packed away all the emotions that Picasso had pulled out of me and readied myself for what I needed to do. This is who I was and the life I chose for myself, no point in thinking of what could have been. Reaching the basement, I saw the delivery man was indeed awake and thrashing in his bindings. When he saw me, his eyes went wide and he struggled even harder, but the leather restraints wouldn't budge.

I walked over to the counter and pulled open a drawer, revealing a pair of thin spandex gloves with a coated palm for extra grip. Slipping them on, I then grabbed a few other items I thought I might need depending on how much trouble this guy was going to cause me. Selecting one of my thin knives, I walked over to the man, flipping the knife and watching his eyes track the weapon.

"Hello, I don't think we were properly introduced. I'm Dax. I know you're wondering why on earth you've been brought down here and strapped to a chair. The thing is, the owner of Lucifer's and I have an arrangement that Tino is always the one who delivers to me. Unfortunately, I have some major trust issues and just can't stand the thought of unknown people knowing where I live. So imagine my surprise when you showed up with a gun hidden in with my order." I bent over so we were eye level. "I'm sure you can see the dilemma here."

The man nodded his head and tried to talk around the gag, but nothing he said was decipherable. Reaching around, I unhooked the gag and let it fall from his mouth as I brought my knife up to his throat.

"Okay, let's try that again, and let's be honest the first time around. I'm not really in the mood to torture you tonight," I sighed.

"Look, I had no idea that this was your house. I was given instructions to take out the driver and to take the pizza to the address. Then I was supposed to grab a girl named Harper and bring her back to another location," the man blurted, panic bright in his eyes and sweat pouring off his brow.

My blood ran cold at his words. I wasn't their target—Harper was, and I just sent her home.

"Who gave you these orders?" I demanded through

clenched teeth.

"I don't know, honestly. I was given a burner phone and told to wait for instructions. I didn't have a choice. I was short on my sales, and when I couldn't pay my part, they were going to kill me, so when they offered me the chance to do a job with no questions asked, I took it," the man babbled.

I growled at the man, letting my knife dig into his fleshy neck. "Tell me who your drug boss is, then. I also want the location that you were going to take Harper to once you grabbed her."

"Little Fingers is who I deal for," the man squeaked out. "If you pull the phone out of my pocket, you'll find the address they texted me. Please, I just needed to clear my debt, I didn't mean to get mixed up with Two Tricks."

"How do you know that I work for Two Tricks?" I barked, grabbing his throat with my hand and squeezing. I was too mad to use my knife and end up killing him accidentally.

Gargling, the man tried to answer, but my grip was too tight. Letting up slightly, he wheezed out the answer that would change everything.

"Mastiff knows you're working with the Phantom Saints, so he sided with the De León cartel and they're coming for you, then Two Tricks..."

The man might have had more to tell me, but in my rage, I screamed out, letting my knife slice easily across his neck. Needing to do something with my anger, I stabbed him in the chest until I was out of breath. Gasping for air, I shook back my blood-soaked hair when I heard a sound. Looking over to my left, I saw Picasso standing at the bottom of the stairs, horror written all over his face.

"Dax—what have you done?"

"Putting the stamp of approval on the deal between you and Tricks. You've gotten what you wanted, Picasso. Now it's time to see just how far you'll go to keep everyone safe," I said, tossing the dagger and watching it bury itself into the wall as I walked over to the shower I had installed for easy cleanup.

Stripping out of my bloody clothes, I turned the water as hot as it could go and stepped under the stream. The water ran red as I scrubbed my body, removing all traces of what had just happened in this room.

"I don't understand, Dax. Who the fuck is—was—that guy? How did he even get down here? Was he trapped here the whole time you were gone?" Picasso demanded, his tone full of self-righteous indignation.

Rinsing the soap from my hair, I charged at him, finger pointed right in his bitch-ass face. "That man was here to kidnap Harper and use her against ME! It seems we have a rat in both our groups, because your pal Mastiff knows that we are hanging around each other and assumed that meant we teamed up. Now the De León cartel and the Mad Dogs have started their own partnership, and that means we are completely and utterly FUCKED!"

Picasso stepped back at the venom in my words, looking back at the man I killed, slumped and covered in blood. "You didn't have to kill him—he didn't do the job. He could have just run or gone into hiding."

"God! WAKE THE FUCK UP, Picasso!" I screamed. "We're at war, and that is only the first of the deaths that will be on both our hands. This is what it means to do what is necessary to keep our people safe. Do what you want with the situation, but I need to go find out if they sent another person after my friend. If they did, I'll kill that motherfucker too."

Chapter Twenty-Nine
Dax

Walking into my closet with a towel wrapped around my hair, I pulled all the clothes in the very back to the side, revealing large gun safe. Swiftly, I unlocked it and took stock of what I had available to me even though I knew every single item in here like the back of my hand. Pulling out my favorite pair of Smith & Wesson handguns, I pulled the slide back, double-checking there was one in the chamber as I slid home the clip.

Setting them aside, I pulled on my black jeans and a simple black t-shirt before slipping on the shoulder holster, making sure it was adjusted so it wouldn't flop around under my jacket. Then I put on my thigh holster that would hold my second gun and two knives. Grabbing two extra clips for each gun, I packed those into the pouch on the small of my back. Finishing off, I slipped on fingerless gloves that had metal reinforcements on the knuckles.

Snatching up my steel-toed combat boots, I glared down

at the monitor on my ankle, cursing its existence. Reaching into my nightstand, I pulled out my inner earpiece that Weston would be able to connect to with his phone. I hit his speed dial, and it took three rings for him to answer.

"Dax, what's wrong," Wes asked, sounding like he'd been awake.

"I need you to pull up the tracker on Harper and tell me where she is. Then I need you to look up everything you know about the drug dealer Little Fingers and if he has ties to the De León cartel or the Mad Dogs," I instructed as I shrugged on my leather jacket.

"Care to give me a hint on what's got you in Terminator mode?" Wes asked. I could already hear him typing.

"Seems that we have a leak in the boat, and someone came up with the bright idea to go after Harper to get to me. Oh, and tell Eagle that the deal is on. Now that the De León cartel and Mastiff have joined forces against Tricks, we are gonna need all the help we can get," I answered, hurrying down the stairs. "Got a location for me yet?"

"Yeah, looks like she's at home. I'm checking her security real quick to make sure she doesn't have any unwanted company."

I knew this day would come, and in preparation I made sure that I had eyes and ears on Harper at all times. Under the guise of needing a person to practice piercing on, I put a tracker in the jewelry I used. Thankfully, your conch wasn't something you changed the stud on often. Wes also talked her into letting him set up her home security so we could set it up with two systems—one for us and the other that she could use like normal. Harper was far too pure and trusting to land in this darkness, and I would be damned if anyone fucked that up for her.

"I got six guys at the house; it looks like Harper is tied to a chair in her kitchen. With the state of the house, she didn't go down without a fight. Those self-defense classes you gave her might be the only reason they didn't get a chance to take her somewhere else yet," Wes relayed. "Two are talking to her in the kitchen while the others are guarding the front and back doors. When you hit the house, be ready for a real fight on your hands, because these guys look professional."

"Got it. I'm sending you the address for the location they were supposed to bring her once caught. I'll check back in once I've got Harper," I said, hanging up and hitting the button for the garage door.

Seeing Picasso already there leaning against his bike, I raised an eyebrow.

"You didn't really think I was going to let you go on your own to deal with this, did you?" he challenged.

Grabbing my helmet off the shelf, I tucked it under my arm as I walked over to him. "After the display down in the basement, I wasn't sure you would even still be here, to be honest. Thought I might have pushed you too far out of your rose-colored world."

"Dax, I'm not blind, I just choose not to let the evil in this world get its claws deeper into my life than I have to. Respecting life shouldn't be seen as a weakness," Picasso said with a shrug.

"If you're going to play in my world it is. So either find your balls and get the fuck on the bandwagon or go home. I can't worry about keeping you alive when Harper is my priority," I snapped as I pulled on my helmet, effectively ending the discussion.

Seconds later I was flying full throttle though the city streets of L.A., weaving around cars, ignoring stop lights, and praying that I wouldn't be too late. My hope was that they would see her value in drawing me out rather than trying to get information out of her. I still had the element of surprise on my side—they had no clue about her added security that was strictly known between Wes and me.

Picasso was right on my heels, leaving me impressed that he had the guts to pull the same reckless shit I did. What normally was a thirty-minute drive was cut down to fifteen after disregarding all traffic laws. As we got to her neighborhood, I made sure to park two streets over, killing the engine as we coasted closer. Thankfully she lived off a busier street, so traffic noise at this time of night wasn't as noticeable. Stashing my helmet, I pulled one of my guns as I waited for Picasso to join me. I was pleased when I saw he too had a gun in his grip.

Maybe there was a chance he could survive this war.

I motioned for him to follow me as we headed for the back of the house. Harper was lucky enough to get this amazing bungalow with an upper loft that she inherited from her grandparents. Even better, it had a large yard with a bunch of fruit trees on the property to give us coverage. Once in the trees and as close as we could get, I reached up to my earpiece and tapped it twice.

"Go ahead. I cut the motion sensors and the floodlight to the backyard. The window sensors say that her bedroom window is open. The guys inside haven't changed positions," Wes informed me.

Tapping the earpiece again, I turned to Picasso. "I'm going in through her bedroom window upstairs. When I get the drop on the guys by the front door, that will draw the rest of them so you can sneak in the back door and get Harper the hell out of there. Take her back to the compound and I'll catch up with you guys once I deal with these assholes."

"Fuck, Dax, you can't take them all on. That's suicidal," Picasso hissed.

"That's the plan. If you don't like it, then leave now, but I'm going to save my best friend," I growled and headed off.

Keeping to the shadows, I followed along the trees as far as they would take me. Darting to the bushes that edged the house, I climbed the ivy-covered lattice up to the second floor. There was a small overhang just under Harper's bedroom window, giving me a perch to stand on as I used my knife to pop out her screen. Dropping to the floor in her room, I stashed the knife and pulled my gun once again.

Crouched low, I moved my way across the room until I could peer through the railing of the stairs to see two guys in suits with guns watching the front of the house. The way the house was set up, everything on the first level was a fairly open concept, with the kitchen as the central location. Ever so slowly, I stood, took aim, and shot the first guy, quickly followed by the second, both head shots.

"Fuck, someone's in the house!" one guy called, rushing into the living room. I picked him off next.

"Second floor!"

A shot went off, and I got clipped on the left thigh from one of them hiding behind the couch. It wasn't a great angle, which is what saved me from getting shot worse. Returning fire, I got him in the shoulder, but he ducked down before I could get off a second shot. I needed to move now that they knew I was up here. Sliding down the wall, I crouched and hobbled down the stairs as my leg burned with the skin getting pulled around the wound. When I reached the landing that would put me right out in the open, I took a few deep breaths and dashed forward, vaulting over the railing as two more shots were fired. I landed and rolled out of the way, behind a large, overstuffed armchair that had been knocked over.

Peeking out, I saw the guy behind the couch pop his head up, and this time I didn't miss my mark.

Four down, two to go.

"Dax, I presume," a voice called out from the direction of the back sunroom.

Shifting, I darted over to hide behind the loveseat to get a better angle to see who was talking. There I found, standing with a gun to Harper's head, a large bald man dressed in jeans, a t-shirt, and a leather vest. The patch on his cut told me he was part of the Mad Dogs MC, confirming what the dead guy in my basement said.

Harper was in her pajamas, the oversized shirt falling off one shoulder where it was torn. She had a black eye and a split lip, causing my anger to ratchet up to an even higher level. There would be no survivors tonight.

"Come on out now, I've traveled so far in the hopes of meeting you, Dax. The least you can do is have a chat with me—or do you need more motivation?" the man said, jerking his head at someone I couldn't see.

An equally substantial man with a mullet dragged an unconscious Picasso by the back of his shirt, a large revolver in the other hand. Did the Mad Dogs only recruit giants? These assholes were ridiculous.

"Still not enough?" the bald man taunted. "Alright then, on the count of three, I'll shoot one of them in the head, but I'm not going to tell you which one."

"One...Two..."

Gritting my teeth so hard my jaw started to ache, I stood up from behind the loveseat, gun at the ready.

A smile broke out over the bald man's face as he took me in. "Pint-sized and deadly, just as described. I have to say, it's a real honor to meet you. I'm a huge fan of your work. See, I'm an enforcer as well—name's Doc."

"Hmm, can't say that I've ever heard of you," I replied.

"Ha! She's got jokes, Goliath." Doc laughed, as did his companion. "This is gonna be way more fun than I thought. Here's the thing. Mastiff is also a long-time fan; he's been tracking you since you helped Two Tricks take his place in the underworld. The Mad Dogs had plans, but it seems that the Phantom Saints have once again moved in on our turf."

"What the fuck does that even mean?" I asked, cocking my head to the side.

"The partnership that you have with the Saints should be with us. We never wanted to work with the De León cartel, but we needed to do something to get your attention. The thing we didn't factor in was Diego was pinning a murder on you to cause strife in your empire and to get rid of a rebellion in his own family," Doc rambled on.

"Are we getting to the point where I come in soon, or is that gonna be a while?" I sighed, using my gun to scratch my head.

Doc shook his gun at me. "Now, now, none of that. I do enjoy a sharp tongue on a woman, but I hate to be interrupted. Letting me say my piece will keep your friends alive and speed things along."

Proving a point, I holstered my gun and walked around the loveseat to sit on the coffee table, one leg crossed over the other and my chin resting on my hand. To them I looked bored and relaxed, but it gave me perfect access to the knives and gun in my thigh holster if I needed to move quickly.

"As I was saying, now that we are stuck in this deal with the De Leóns, they are holding us by our balls. We would so much rather work with *you,* and Two Tricks, of course.

After all, you were promised to us ages ago," Doc stated, causing me to gawk at him.

"Let me tell you a little secret about your brother and his lovely wife." The smug look on his face told me that I wasn't going to like one word of what he was going to share. "When your twin got out of jail and was kicked to the curb, he tried everything to get back in their good graces, even offering you as an incentive. They turned him down, so the lovely Kimber came to us asking if we would take over the Blackjax in retribution. Oh, and they kept you part of the deal as well. Sadly, before any of this could happen, your brother was gunned down in a drug deal gone wrong. Imagine my surprise when his twin sister who was promised to us makes her splash into the dark world by helping Two Tricks wipe out an MC."

My stomach rolled at the thought of my brother, my twin, the other part of my soul, selling me out. I knew it was Kimber's doing if it was true at all. She's always hated me.

"Mastiff wanted to take you from Two Tricks quickly, but we ran into our own troubles and had to leave. We always kept an eye on you though, Dax, watching you turn into a beautiful deadly weapon." Doc grinned at me like a proud parent. "As you can see, you were promised to the Mad Dogs. It's where you belong. So we need you to drop the Phantom Saints and then kill off Diego so we are free of him. Simple, really. I know what you're thinking—how can we ask you to do this when you don't trust us or know what we have to offer? It's simple—we aren't asking."

What the fuck kind of bullshit was this man spewing?

I let the silence hang in the air as I just watched him, not reacting to what he just said. Inside I was seething. How the fuck could they think they could walk into my city, hold my friend at gunpoint, and expect me to just do or believe what they say? Some fans they were—clearly they hadn't been paying attention, and now they done fucked up.

"Let me see if I've got this right. You're butt hurt because you acted too rashly and got into a bad deal with a known two-timing bastard. Twice, now that I think about it, when you include that skank Kimber—if any of that is even true. Sounds to me like your problems are a result of your own poor choices. Boo hoo," I said, giving him an exaggerated pout. "Whoever your mole or moles are didn't do a very good job getting you accurate facts on the situation between the Phantom Saints and myself. I didn't agree to work with them until I found out that my best friend was being targeted."

Doc opened his mouth to speak, but I held up a hand. "Shhh, I'm not done talking yet."

I couldn't help but smirk at the vein that started throbbing on his big shiny forehead.

"I'm glad you're not asking, because no matter what you do or say, there is not a flaming fart of a chance that I will ever work with drool hounds like yourself. Now that we have that all cleared up, what happens next?" I asked, raising a brow at him.

Doc gave away his intentions with the evil glint in his eyes, and before I could question myself, I acted. Drawing my gun with my left hand and a knife in my right, I shot Doc between his eyes and threw my knife at Goliath. It landed in his chest, and it threw him off balance long enough that I was able to get my next shots off into his heart. Harper screamed and crumpled to the floor, scrambling away from Doc as his blood started to seep out on the tile.

Rushing forward, I dropped my gun and grabbed Harper, who then clung to me, sobbing into my chest.

"I got you, Harper. I got you. You're safe now. I'm so

sorry I wasn't here faster," I murmured as I stroked her head, rocking her as she cried.

Mastiff fucked with the wrong person, and he was going to figure that out very soon, because I was going to destroy him and everyone around him.

Chapter Thirty
Weston

Falling back against the couch, I let out the breath that I'd been holding since Dax entered the house. Thanks to the security system, I had been able to watch and listen to the whole thing as it was going down. Seeing my woman in her element was something I never got tired of, but this one was far too close to home, having Harper involved.

Seeing her wrapped around Dax as her body shook with sobs made it hard for me not to head straight to the closest Mad Dog crew and kill every one of them. Not only had they been after Dax, they'd used the one person who was her true weakness. I had no doubt that she would do anything to get me back if need be, but if she lost Harper, it would break the last part of her innocence.

"So is no one is going to bring it up?" Cognac asked, breaking my train of thought.

I looked over my laptop screen at the other four guys, who'd been watching everything on the TV before I cut the link off, wanting to give Harper some privacy. Once Dax had called and let me know what was going down, I woke up everyone else and gathered them here. They wanted to go after Dax, but I knew they wouldn't get there in time for it to matter. Situations like this were what Dax lived for, and she was good at it.

"Bring what up?" Eagle snapped, glaring at Cognac. "If you say something asinine, I'm going to punch you in the nuts."

He was the one I almost had to tackle and tie to a chair to keep him from going after Dax and his brother, but Sprocket talked him down. Void wasn't much better, but he wouldn't go without Eagle.

"Our woman just took out six armed men and saved two hostages single-handedly. She's like a live version of Lara Croft or some shit," Cognac said as he stood, looking down at the other three. "You're telling me you didn't realize that if she really wanted to get the fuck out of here, she could have? So why didn't she?" Cognac asked.

After a moment, they all looked at me like I was just going to give them the answer. "Oh no, you guys either need to figure it out yourselves or ask her, but I'm not gonna tell you if you don't already know."

"I think that is a conversation for another time. Right now we need to prepare for the war that is about to descend on us," Sprocket interjected before Eagle could try and wring the answer from me.

Looking back at my screen, I saw Dax wrapping a blanket around Harper and then heading over to Picasso, who was still out cold. Dragging him away from the very dead Goliath, she checked him over carefully, but from what I saw he'd just been pistol-whipped. Once she was convinced he would be alright, she went back to Harper.

"Babe, I'm gonna pack you a bag and we are gonna stay

with some friends of mine. I promise I will explain everything once we get there, but we need to move before any more bad guys show up," Dax explained in a soft voice.

Harper didn't really react to what Dax said as she kept picking at the tassels on the blanket. Letting out a sigh, Dax left her and headed up to Harper's room. Now that she was alone, I felt comfortable enough to call out to her. Hitting the button that would activate my side of the comms, I tapped twice.

"Wondered how long it would take you to reach out," Dax said, glancing up at the camera. "You catch all that went down?"

"Yeah, I made sure to record the audio so we could go back over it once you didn't have Harper's life hanging in the balance," I assured her.

Nodding, she kept moving around the room. "Can I assume the rest of the guys are with you too?"

"You would assume correct, little hellcat," Eagle called out, "and you got one hell of a punishment waiting for you when you get back for pulling a stunt like that."

"Fuck off Eagle," Dax snapped. "If you were paying attention at all, you'd know it's your fault I'm even in this situation."

Eagle scoffed. "Then we must have been listening to two different conversations, because it sounded like if we didn't come along, the same thing would have happened but with the Mad Dogs. They aren't as hospitable as we are, to say the least."

"Why don't we have this conversation a little later in person," Dax grumbled. "I somehow have to get my catatonic best friend and your unconscious brother out of here and back to the compound in a Fiat, and then figure out what the fuck to do with our bikes."

"Just get back here, rebel. Bikes can be replaced, but you guys can't," Sprocket said.

They couldn't see, but Dax flipped off the camera, and I just smiled. "She gave a thumbs up."

"I'll just bet she did." Void smirked.

"We'll see you when you get here," I said as I signed off Harper's system.

I looked at the guys, who looked far more haggard than I was, not used to dealing with this lifestyle. "At this point, you have two choices—make more coffee or try and catch an hour of sleep before she gets here."

"I'll get the coffee brewing," Sprocket said as he heaved himself off the couch.

Eagle rubbed his jaw, deep in thought, while the other two seemed to wait on his direction. This was the biggest difference between how they worked and how Dax and I worked—we were a team. Both of us had strengths that the other didn't, and we found a way to blend them to work in the best way possible. These bikers needed instruction before they could move forward, not having the autonomy to just pick up a lead and run it down. As they waited for their leader to make up his mind about whatever it was he was thinking about, I pulled up the file on Little Fingers that I hadn't had a chance to read through yet.

This situation was turning out to have several layers to it, and I just couldn't seem to see where they all intersected. The cleanup crew I sent to the house gave me the information on the man that Dax interrogated, but he was nothing but a low-level dealer. Little Fingers, on the other hand, was middle management, so the task at hand was to see who he reported to. I needed the top of the food chain to get the full picture.

"So at what point does the elusive Two Tricks deem it

necessary to involve himself?" Eagle asked, drawing my attention.

"Oh, he's been involved through this whole situation. I've been keeping him well informed," I answered.

Eagle grunted and leaned forward on his knees. "See, I'm having a hard time believing that a man as powerful as him is still keeping to the shadows with all this. War with a cartel and a biker gang is not a small problem."

I glanced up at him, keeping my expression neutral as my anger flared at what I thought he was hinting at. "Are you saying Tricks is a coward?"

"How would I know?" Eagle challenged. "The man never shows his face and uses proxies for all his deals, so who's to say he's even alive? With a ghost like that, he could be anyone—even you, Weston."

Giving him a smirk, I set my laptop to the side. "And if I was Two Tricks, what then? Does it change the situation we're in or what needs to happen next?"

Void growled at my tone and moved towards me, but Eagle held out a hand, stopping him. "True as that may be, if we are going to war with you, I think it's only fair that I meet the man I'm asking my people to possibly die protecting."

Nodding in agreement, I decided to compromise. "I am not Two Tricks, and as for who that is, it's only fair to have everyone here for that conversation."

"Fine, if we are going to do this, I'll make us something to eat. No telling how fast things will move once Mastiff finds out Doc is dead." Eagle headed into the kitchen, grabbing the coffee cup from Sprocket as he passed.

Sprocket rolled his eyes and went back to make himself a new mug, and I went to pick up my laptop when a shadow loomed over me. Looking up, I found Void standing over me. I quirked an eyebrow at him, waiting for him to speak.

"In the spirit of partnership, I feel that I should tell you that once my little demon is back in this house, I'm not letting her leave us again. She belongs with us whether she realizes it or not. Know that if you try to take her from me and mine, I will not hesitate to kill you, even if it means she will hate me forever," Void warned.

"Dax was never going to be mine alone—she couldn't handle that type of relationship. You may think you can keep her against her will, but if she doesn't want to stay, she won't—and there is no way in hell I'll let you do that to her. If you don't keep her from me, then I won't keep her from you—fair?" I countered, holding out my hand.

Void wrapped his large hand around mine and squeezed hard enough that I was concerned he might break my hand. "Don't make me have to hurt you and everything will be fine."

Having got that off his chest, he headed upstairs.

"So dramatic—am I right?" Cognac said, grinning at me.

I shook my head and got back to work on the matters at hand, knowing Dax would be a tornado of pent-up rage when she got here.

Chapter Thirty-One
Dax

It took longer than I would have liked to get everything settled so we could leave, but I had to go back and grab our bikes and stash them in Harper's garage. I disabled the garage door and took the keys with me, so it would hopefully keep anyone from messing with them. Putting Harper in the joke of a back seat, still bundled in her blanket, I then maneuvered Picasso into the front passenger seat.

Leaning against the car, I called Brian.

"Dax! God, I've been so worried about you—you dropped off the face of the earth," Brian blurted when he answered.

"I'm all good, just needed to deal with some stuff on the down low. Look, I don't have a lot of time to explain things, but I need you to spread the word that Diego De León has teamed up with the Mad Dogs MC and they're gunning for us," I explained.

The silence on the other end had me frowning.

"Does this mean it's true that you took out his kid?"

"No, Brian, I didn't take out his kid. I didn't even know he had one," I said through my teeth. "They are spreading rumors to stir shit up in our house, and seeing how you are questioning me on this, I'd say it's working. Tell me, Brian—you still with me, or do I need to consider this your resignation?"

Everyone knew that when you were in as deep as Brian, there was no leaving the empire alive. I liked him because he was a good guy and did his job perfectly, but I couldn't have someone so high up questioning things when we were headed for war.

"If what you're telling me is that they killed Jeff just to make us doubt you, then I'm all in. His wife just had their first kid, you know. He didn't deserve to go like that. Hell, it could have been me they picked to make an example out of. Don't worry Dax, I got your back. I trust you to tell me what I need to know. Now what can I do for you?" Brian asked, his tone all business.

"I need you to send a cleanup crew to the address I send you, and I need you to oversee them personally. The Mad Dogs went after someone very important to me, and I need to make sure that this is handled with the utmost care so nothing falls back on her," I instructed.

"Sure thing, boss. Sounds like you've been busy—two cleanups in one night. They're not fucking around, are they," Brian sighed.

"No, they sure aren't. I'll have more information for you in the next twenty-four hours. They wanted a war, they're gonna get one. They're gonna regret the day they fucked with my people," I growled and hung up.

Rubbing my forehead, I took a moment before I slid into the car and started it up. I glanced back at Harper, who met my eyes with a little more life in them. I smiled, and she gave me a half-hearted one in return, letting me know that I hadn't lost her completely.

I'd never been a fan of her tiny little car, but as we wove through traffic, I was starting to appreciate its value. The sky was starting to lighten slightly with dawn approaching, and I was even more thankful to get out of the city before the rest of the world woke up. Once on the more open, rural roads, it was smooth sailing. The quiet in the car was relaxed, and I left it that way.

"Ugh," Picasso groaned as he started to wake up, rubbing the back of his head. "Why does my head hurt so much? Wait, why the fuck am I in a clown car?"

Looking at him out of the corner of my eye, I smirked. "It seems we need to work on your infiltration skills. Nothing like a pistol whip to the head to make a great story for your first hostage rescue."

Picasso glared at me, then he caught sight of Harper in the back seat and relaxed a little. "Looks like you weren't lying when you said you didn't need my help."

"Hey, I tried to tell you this isn't my first rodeo. The cesspool of people I have to deal with puts you in all kinds of situations. You have to learn to manage. Six on one is a personal favorite of mine—it makes it challenging enough that I have to actually try," I gloated.

"Dax, are you saying this is normal for you?" Harper whispered, her eyes wide in horror.

The grin on my face fell as fear grew in my heart that she might never look at me the same after this conversation. "This is something I wish you never had to learn about me, Harper. I did everything I could to keep you clear of all this. I promise, once we are safe and you get some rest, I will answer any questions you have, if you want to ask them."

She turned her gaze away from me but didn't say

anything more. Once again, the car fell into silence, but this time it wasn't so comfortable. I pressed the gas down further, needing to get free from the tension that was building in the small space.

As I pulled up right in front of Eagle's house, I wasn't surprised to see all the lights on, a beacon guiding me back. The internal sigh of relief to be back caught me by surprise as I opened my door. Picasso carefully unfolded himself from the small space, trying not to hit his head again. The front door opened a few moments later, Wes and Eagle coming out to meet us.

They both made a beeline right to me, but I waved them off, not wanting their attention. Wes sighed and went to Harper, tucking her under his arm and bringing her into the house. Eagle glared at me, letting me know this wasn't over as he grabbed his brother by the back of his neck and pulled him into a strange bro hug.

Exhausted but knowing that sleep wasn't coming any time soon, I trudged up the steps, where I found Sprocket holding the door open for me. I smiled at him when I saw the coffee mug in his hand that he held out. Cupping it with two hands, I let the heat of the cup revive me, giving me the push to keep going.

Sprocket pulled me to the coffee table, where he sat me down. I raised a brow at him, but he just signaled for me to wait. Not having the energy to argue, I just sipped on my coffee and looked around for Cognac and Void, but I didn't see either. After a minute, Sprocket returned with a large first aid kit and started pulling things out that he needed.

"Pants off," he instructed.

"Gosh, buy a girl dinner first, would ya," I teased, feeling a little punch drunk.

His green eyes held mine, and I saw there was no humor in his gaze. What I found surprised me—Sprocket was angry. Setting my mug down, I stood, undoing my thigh holster and setting it to the side before shimmying off my jeans. I hissed I peeled the fabric off my thigh, the dried blood caused the material to stick to the skin around my injury. It started bleeding again, making Sprocket's frown deepen.

He moved with practiced ease as he cleaned the wound, not speaking a word to me. His touch was gentle but thorough.

"Looks like it's gonna need stitches," Sprocket said, still refusing to look at me as he grabbed more supplies.

I sighed, knowing this was going to burn like a bitch, but it wasn't the first time this had happened in my life, nor would it be the last.

"You any good at those?" I asked. "If not, I can do it myself."

That got Sprocket's attention, his eyes snapping up to mine. "How many times?"

"What?" I asked, wrinkling my brow.

"How. Many. Times. Have you had to stitch yourself up?" Sprocket asked, anger burning in his tone.

"I don't know—I've lost count. It's really not that big of a deal, Sprocket. It happens," I said with a shrug, not understanding why he was so bothered by this.

A growl fell from his lips as he stood and walked away from me towards the bottom of the stairs. "WESTON! Get your ass down here right now!"

I stood from the coffee table, but he whipped around so fast I froze.

"Sit. The. Fuck. Down, Dax," Sprocket demanded.

The fury in his eyes caused me to sink back down, completely caught off guard by what was going on. Wes charged down the stairs, his eyes scanning the room, looking for what could have caused Sprocket to holler for him. Before I could get out a word of warning, Sprocket clocked Weston right in the face, making him stumble into the wall.

"What the fuck, man?!" Wes snarled.

"How could you let her get into situations where she ends up getting hurt and having to patch herself up?! Where the fuck were you? I thought you two were a team, but it sounds to me like you hide safely behind that goddamn screen while she puts her life on the line," Sprocket fumed.

Their argument seemed to draw everyone out, and now all the guys were standing at different points around the room, watching everything unfold. Even Harper was observing from the top stair, clutching a pillow, eyes glued on what was happening before her.

"You have no fucking clue what you're talking about here, asshole," Weston shot back.

Eagle stepped in as Sprocket was about to lunge at Wes again, holding him back with a hand to the chest. "Easy, we need his mouth to keep working so he can explain himself."

Sprocket growled but backed off as the rest of them circled around Wes.

"I think you better enlighten us there, Westical, before Void decides to make good on that threat from earlier," Cognac said, crossing his arms over his chest.

Wes glared at all of them before his gaze flicked to me as if unsure of what he was about to say next. "You guys don't understand, I've been at her side through *everything*. The history that we have both shared and survived in the Hidden

Empire gives me a level of knowledge you will never know. Dax is a survivor and doesn't need a bunch of meat-headed men trying to smother her in a bubble. If she tells me she can handle something, then I let her—but I wouldn't hesitate jumping in front of a bullet for her if the need arose."

"No," Sprocket snapped, getting all up in Weston's face again. "You claim to love her, but from where I'm standing, I don't see it. No woman of mine would be allowed to put her life on the line for me or anyone else. I don't give a fuck who Two Tricks really is, but he's not having her back after this, and neither are you!" Sprocket bellowed.

Weston, having had enough, tackled Sprocket, causing Void to wade into the fight. The blur of fists and grunts as they landed on each other made Harper break.

"Stop!" Harper screamed, running down to the bottom of the stairs where Cognac stopped her. "Please, you have to stop them. They'll kill each other if they keep going!" Tears streamed down her face as she fought against Cognac's hold.

That did it. I shot to my feet, grabbed my gun, and fired a shot into the floor. This caused the room to fall silent as they looked at me with shocked faces. Marching over to them, I watched as they scrambled to their feet, Wes wiping at his bloody nose while Sprocket looked like he might have a black eye. Void even got a split lip out of the exchange.

"Are you dumbasses finished? Let's start with the fact that Wes couldn't have stopped me if he wanted to—he doesn't own me or control me. If you lot think you're going to have a better shot at it than him, I'll tell you right now that it's not gonna happen. Now that that's clear—do you really think you could take me away from Tricks?" I demanded, hands on my hips. The guys frowned at my words, chomping at the bit to tell me they could. "I got news for you dipshits—*I'm motherfucking Two Tricks!*"

At my declaration, the room stilled, all eyes trained on me as my words hit home.

"Joke's on you, idiots. The one person you've been trying so desperately to get the attention of has been sitting right in fucking front of you. Weston is my right-hand man, as well as my best friend, but when it comes to the Hidden Empire, he works for me! If he tried to keep me from doing what is necessary, I could have cut him off and out of my life. He keeps his mouth shut and lets me put my life at risk, no matter how much he hates it, because I always come back," I snarled, my breathing heavy with the flood of emotions that was hitting me. "Now back the FUCK off of him."

Void tilted his head back and began to laugh a deep belly laugh. "Oh, little demon, you are the best surprise I could have asked for in life."

This seemed to break the tension in the room, and I noticed that Harper was gone from the stairs. I groaned to myself, knowing that was the worst way possible for her to hear this. Flopping down on the coffee table once more, I hung my head in my hands and fisted my fingers in my hair. God, how was I ever going to fix this?

Hands covered my own, pulling them from my hair, causing me to look up and see Weston squatting in front of me. "Don't write her off just yet, shortcake. Trust in your friendship. Harper knows the real you that no one else gets to see, just give her time to take it all in. This has been a rough night for everyone."

I nodded and gave him a weak smile, and he stepped aside for Sprocket to get back to my wound. He had to clean it all over again, seeing as I couldn't keep still and caused it to start weeping again.

Once ready, he looked up at me. "I'm sorry I lost it like that, little rebel, I just couldn't stand the thought of you having to deal with this all on your own. We good?"

"I don't know... are we good? If you're pissed at me, I think I'd rather do this myself then have you make this hurt worse than it already will," I said.

Sprocket cupped my face and rested his forehead against mine. "You did what you needed to survive, who am I to judge? Besides, it's kinda cool that I have the most powerful woman on the West Coast right in front of me. Queen of the Hidden Empire, woman of the Phantom Saints leadership. How people will talk."

I narrowed my eyes at him. "I don't remember signing up to be your woman or anyone else's."

"Hmm, you're right. That doesn't quite seem to work, does it? How about this. The Queen of the Hidden Empire and her knights willing to defend her at any cost," Sprocket mused.

"You sure you can speak for the others like that, road captain?" I teased.

Pressing a soft kiss to my lips, Sprocket leaned back, letting me see everyone else gathered on the couch before me.

"Anyone disagree?" Sprocket asked, turning to look at them.

"Nope, every queen needs strong knights to keep her in line," Eagle said with a twinkle in his eyes.

"I've always wanted to be a knight!" Cognac piped up, a wide smile on his lips.

"Seems like our little vixen is stuck with us," Picasso smirked.

Void grunted, crossing his arms as he met my gaze. "You guys make it seem like she had a choice. My little demon wasn't ever going to leave us again."

Finally, I looked at Wes, knowing there was so much we hadn't had a chance to talk about, but if I was honest with myself, I knew all along we would end up here.

"Dax, my love and loyalty has always been yours, and if you decide these guys are yours too, then that's all I need to know," Wes assured me.

"It's settled then. Two Tricks has an alliance with the Phantom Saints that *she* will personally oversee. Now Sprocket, if you could be so kind as to stitch me up, we have a war to prepare for," I announced, grinning at my guys.

ELIZABETH KNIGHT

Elizabeth is originally from Illinois but is now living in the sunny Phoenix AZ. Though she is newer to publishing, Elizabeth has been writing for nine years. She started out in YA Fiction but recently found herself loving the Reverse Harem genre. Like her favorite books, Elizabeth loves to write strong women of all varieties. Not all strength is flashy or apparent at first glance—some lies just under the surface.

Don't Miss Out!

Be the first to know what is coming next by following Elizabeth's social media! You never know when or what will be coming next!

ALSO BY ELIZABETH KNIGHT

Elementi Series

Book 1 - Discovering Synergy

Book 2 – Refining Earth

Book 3 – Liberating Water April 4th, 2021

Hope Series

Book 1 – Hidden Hope

Book 2 – Claiming Hope

Book 3 – Defending Hope June 20th, 2021

Mercenary Queen Series

Book 1 – Birthright

Book 2 - Dragon Queen Sept. 19th 2021

Hidden Empire Series

Book 1 - Two Tricks

Some Kind of Luck

The Trouble with Luck (Some Kind of Luck Book 1 – Co-write) March 17th 2021

Stroke of Luck (Some kind of Luck Book 3) August 29 2021

Printed in Great Britain
by Amazon